D1797814

Jon Cocks is a long-serving Drama and English teacher. Other than an enduring love affair with wife Lilit, his passions include books, Australian football, the Adelaide Crows, Australian cricket, theatre, movies and wine. He has an adult son, Jordan. He lives with Lilit in the Adelaide Hills.

For my darling Lilit

Jon Cocks

Duty of Care

AUSTIN MACAULEY
PUBLISHERS LTD.

A CIP catalogue record for this title is available from the British Library.

ISBN 9781786292346 (Paperback)
ISBN 9781786292353 (Hardback)
ISBN 9781786292360 (eBook)
www.austinmacauley.com

First Published (2017)
Austin Macauley Publishers Ltd.
25 Canada Square
Canary Wharf
London
E14 5LQ

Classroom survival is mainly about self belief. Liquid 'professional development' with friends and allies conducted nowhere near a conference room, well away from rubrics, flow charts, proficiency scales, data-rich PowerPoint presentations and well-paid 'trending' consultants...that can help as well...

Thanks to colleagues and friends: Paul Rivers, Brian & Jenni Lannen, Gary Beasley, Adrian Birrell, Peter Moran, the late Tony 'Donk' Chiodo, Brendan Fitzgerald, Ivan Bronsert, Graham Brand, Trent English & Robyn Pine.

Monday, 9.00 a.m.

"Where the bloody hell is he?"

Steve Royston's first two replacements had lasted two days and a half day respectively. The latest was a theoretical entity at best. No unfamiliar sedan rolled speculatively through the Happy Vale High School car park gate. Fifty Year Nines boiled around me: spicy, tart, sweet, sour, robust, subtle, a volatile blend.

Naomi Meredith shook her multi-coloured mop of hair. Her furtive eyes pretended to consult a list as my phone rang. I hurried to the perimeter of the throng and answered.

"Pete," rang the bullish tones of Gazza, a mate from my school days, whose property development business was booming in permanent overdrive. Gaz was a uni dropout whose relentless cash accumulation nowadays made my Education Department salary look like the pittance we made as kids stacking supermarket shelves and serving at Macca's. "Have you thought about my offer?"

"I don't know."

My heart sank.

The unknown terror of sacrificing guaranteed salary with full pay throughout the long holidays on a promise only was daunting. Gazza saw my acting skills as useful in selling his ambitious dreams. What the hell was I doing, still wasting my talent? I could make a fortune, he assured me.

"Pete," the voice in my ear cut through the teen babble, "what's not to know? We've heard about the bullshit at school down the pub often enough. You do the short course before the end of the financial year and I put you in the office. You won't know yourself after a month."

"I don't know," I repeated, internal warning bell clanging at becoming the active dispenser of bullshit, rather than being the passive recipient of it.

"Look, mate, I can't wait forever. I'm gonna need to put *someone* on before long. What's holding you up?"

"I'm about to head off on camp for a week," I said.

It was an answer unrelated to my fear of the financial unknown. It also failed to address the other consequence of leaving Happy Vale after five years, the very real possibility of never seeing Maddy again.

"OK, take the week to think about it. I'll buzz you on Friday. That long enough?" Without giving me time to answer, he hung up.

A week on camp in April with a hundred Year Nines might be a career-affirming challenge to my spirit, as my Arts manager put it, but three hours alone with half of them was still three times the Outdoor Ed teacher-student Duty of Care supervision ratio. Victoria, Tony and Doc had been on Naomi's case for days to find another Outdoor Ed specialist. I noticed Naomi flick an agitated glance at her watch. Admin's all-important Wellness conference week was about to begin, with its ecstasy of insights and paroxysms of paradigm-shifting truths.

In truth, though, only the brightest, most 'well' cherubs, as Doc referred to them, would meet the Minister, dignitaries and mandarins of pedagogy. Their camp photos, local-media-lauded triumphs, YouTube videos and Facebook likes would intoxicate the most ardent publisher of upbeat newsletter items. I had spent Sunday getting drunk. It had not helped me become affirmative about the cherubs our visitors would not meet. It had not helped my wellness, either.

Tony and Doc had already departed on the first bus, apologetic grins acknowledging the potent mix pressure-cooking on the second. Maddy and Victoria had gone ahead earlier to shop for fresh camp supplies. Trust Steve to break his leg just before *this* week, during the fire drill fiasco that definitely did *not* make the newsletter. Steve sniggered to Tony about small mercies through tears of pain. The ambos thought he was delusional and fed him extra pain-killers.

"Peter, you have to leave." Naomi's adenoidal nagging grated through the racket and my hangover. "We'll send him on when he gets here."

"We've got Moon!" sniggered Blake Sims from under the outsized fringe that protruded from his marijuana-motif-bearing baseball cap.

"Moon him when we get on the bus!" enthused Trent Wigmore.

Texting thumbs twiddled new Facebook status entries: 'mooning' Moon, amid hilarious screeching, the mating cry of the Eastern Ranges Galoot, as Doc would define. My head hurt.

"Why can't we have Miss Ambrose?" whined Annika Jones, pink hair fluffing, pink lipstick-lips pouting and pink Ugg boots rippling in the morning breeze, as she eyed me sourly. "She's the Year Nine Co-coordinator. Why do we have to have *him*?"

They all wanted Miss Maddy Ambrose. I was the teacher you were stuck with, when you couldn't have Miss Ambrose. Ironically, no one wanted the divine Miss Ambrose more than I did. From Day One at Happy Vale my heart was hers. I had not stopped longing for the miracle that would open her jewel-like, violet eyes to me.

Naomi retreated, the door opened and the kids swarmed on board.

"Peter," Naomi's first-ever words to me reverberated, as we left school behind. "There's no withdrawal room at Happy Vale. Our children are angels."

The Hell that was my first Drama class still burnt inside, a wall-to-wall cackling, hellish rugby-tackling, waking nightmare. My first English class was a cross between all-in wrestling and indoor cricket, myself an unheeded umpire until I caught the ball. Ron Ferrier eventually appeared with the ball's owner to address the boy's grievance over the theft of his property.

"Russell has made significant progress since last year," Ferrier murmured. "Read his file and develop an alternative learning plan for him."

Ferrier took the ball from my limp fingers and gave it back to Russell. In the herd's departing thunder at recess I tried to make sense of what just happened. At the end of the day - at the end of that year - I was no wiser.

In those days, the philosophy of embroidering Wellness into Brave New Classrooms was but a twinkle in the eyes of enterprising psychologists. Having read many a file and developed a library of alternative learning plans in the meantime, wisdom remained elusive. Five years of alarm distilled to dread, especially since Ferrier had been elevated lately to principal.

"Travis," Annika shrieked. "You fucking dickwad!"

Ever since, as a new Year Eight, Travis Armour told me to go fuck myself, I knew I had a 'live' one. That time Travis decided hang off the lighting bar in the Drama Room, having leapt there via his perch on top of Drama blocks piled precariously for that purpose. His aim was to connect the faulty strobe lamp filched from my office to a power point intended for stage lighting, despite my clear instruction to the contrary. His contempt for my concerns over group health and safety encouraged instant mass disobedience. Somehow I was wrong to prefer a structured introductory lesson on stagecraft to an improvised wild party in a strobe-flickering, otherwise blacked-out Drama studio.

Not long afterwards, on yard duty at the back of the bottom oval, I came upon Travis behind the bushes at his business activities: the exchange of garden shed 'skunk' for meth-amphetamines from two surly individuals who had definitely not passed through the front office to collect their visitors' badges. The suspension that followed had the unfortunate consequence of Travis discovering my home address. Shortly after came the tags on my garage roll-a-door, flat tyres on my car and vandalism of my letterbox. Then I was assaulted outside the pub by the same two individuals who had departed so abruptly that lunchtime, before I had any chance to introduce myself formally. Travis and his associates had attracted the attention of the local constabulary, but had not yet been nabbed red-handed with contraband, blunt object or spray-can in hand.

By some cosmic act of time-tabling serendipity, Travis was now in my Year Nine Care group. The educational gods had pre-ordained our reconciliation. As newly appointed Year Nine Coordinator, Maddy had interceded repeatedly on his behalf, in her unbreakable resolve that there was no such thing as a bad student. Being at odds with her on that tore at my heart. Maddy merely smiled patiently, as if convinced I would learn eventually from my error. However, Travis was one act of destruction or violence away from being locked up in Juvenile Detention, according to our over-worked youth worker.

His latest and current four-week suspension occurred when Tony discovered him in his 'office' at the back of the bottom oval doing business with a few of the more cashed-up Year Eights. Maddy expressed disappointment and recommended forgiveness. Naomi had agitated behind closed doors for inaction, as the event had been largely unnoticed, but Ferrier's usually inert hand was forced by the length of the boy's record.

The Outdoor Ed faculty had conducted a sustained campaign to enforce a permanent school camp ban on Travis after the Year Eight tent fire incident, when he passed out with a lit marijuana pipe in his hand. He had been excluded in Term Four the previous year for throwing the brick through Maddy's classroom window that went centimetres from blinding her and scarred the exquisite perfection of her face. He shouldn't have been anywhere near this excursion. Maddy had already forgiven him. I had not.

And there was Travis, daubing 'war-paint' on his perma-scowl with Annika's lipstick.

"Take us back to school," I demanded of the driver.

"Sorry, mate. I need to be at Wakefield before home time today."

Calling school was as futile as arguing with the bus company's schedule. Besides, the forest had killed reception.

"The moment we get to camp," I growled, "I'll have you removed."

"No fuckin' way, man."

"Move to the front."

"Get fucked."

"Tra-vis! Tra-vis!" chanted the kids.

Damien Zammit offered a sneer from the rear. He had been suspended the previous Friday for lighting a cigarette from a live Bunsen burner in Victoria's Science class and blowing smoke in her face when she failed to appreciate his comic genius. I subsided into my seat.

"Mr Moon?" whispered the diminutive Karen Smithers from the seat behind. "Me 'n' Sarah...we wanted to tell you they sneaked Damien and Travis on the bus, but the others said they'd bash us."

An ironic cheer interrupted my contemplation of Karen's good intentions. We were passing the other bus, held up by a flat tyre. The kids had scattered. Doc and Tony were nowhere to be seen.

"Can we stop to see how long they'll be?"

"No time," the driver grunted. "I'm late for Wakefield as it is.

Monday, 2.00 p.m.

The bus turned off the highway and rumbled several kilometres up a dirt track through the forest to the modern office and bush-set buildings of the Outdoor Education Centre. I tried to call Tony. Reception was still down.

Erupting from the bus like warm Coke from a well-shaken bottle, the kids clattered through the open courtyard, all claiming bunks in the female dorm. A brilliantly red and green rosella parrot landed unexpectedly on my shoulder. The stowaways were not among the milling throng.

"Damien! Travis!"

The bird fluttered away. A head-count had three others missing. In the open cooking area boys were devouring chips and biscuits. Girls milled about in chattering throngs, the excited babble punctuated by screeches of shrill laughter. A food fight broke out.

I spoke in stentorian tones: "Sit down around the campfire space."

Perhaps it was my Satanic mask of rage that drove them to settle in the outdoor communal area adjoining the dorms. Or maybe they thought I'd be distributing lollies. Through the red mist I observed a middle-aged woman enter the clearing, feathers distinctly ruffled.

"Excuse me," she sniffed. "Are you the only adult here? My sister and I were bowled over by some of your boys who were belting along the bush track, without looking at where they were going. They used the most appalling language at us when my sister objected. And they were shooting stones at the rosellas from high-powered shanghais."

Shreds of paper and braying laughter floated past on a gust of wind. Words eluded me. A page slapped into the woman's face.

She removed it and read: "Happy Vale High School..."

It was difficult to determine if her expression denoted pity or contempt. Ferrier was always at us to seek marketing opportunities, to raise the school's profile. This was one way. Doc would enjoy that. Our visitor left as abruptly as she arrived.

"Damien! Travis!"

Almost immediately, Trent, Blake and Tristan came thundering into the gathering. Red fury dissipated into white-hot clarity. The boys sat and the group fell silent. They were probably surprised at the absence of lollies.

"Where are Damien and Travis?"

"Dunno," said Blake blankly.

"This is a wilderness area," I grated. "People who visit this site have a responsibility to keep the environment clean and to leave the wildlife alone."

"It wasn't us –" began Trent.

"Trent. The woman you harassed was just here."

"No way, man –"

"Shut up!" Karen and Sarah, sitting nearest me, stared with open mouths. "You guys have given our school bad press and we haven't been here five minutes. Hand over the shanghais."

"What shanghais?" sneered Tristan.

"The ones you were shooting at the birds with."

"That wasn't us –"

"I will give you exactly one minute to give me the shanghais, or you boys will be sent home in taxis from this campsite and your parents will foot the bill. Five hundred bucks, maybe…"

Gasps were muted. Trent stood and slouched to the clearing's edge. An internal voice nagged on the impossibility of calling parents without a working signal.

"Trent," shouted Blake. "You idiot."

Trent returned with three lethal weapons. The 'Y'-shaped frame of each comprised thick gaffer-taped strands of wire. The projectiles were hurled from a leather cup cut from a used Nike boot's tongue, powered by multiple layers of thick rubber bands, genuinely creative use of the school's tech studies facilities. I dismantled them and dropped their components into a plastic bag as evidence.

"Where are Damien and Travis?"

Blank faces. A long moment of silence. Victoria and Maddy drove into the clearing and pulled up.

"Peter," said Maddy, after I had finished venting. She shot a mocking glance at Victoria. "We're so sorry. But when *someone* ignores the GPS and decides to take what *she* thinks is a short cut, you have to expect delays."

I opened my mouth. No cool witticism emerged to make light of my disquiet. Maddy's mesmerising dark beauty did it to me every time.

"It was a short cut back when I was a uni student." Victoria smiled, her round, honest cheeks blushing. "And I did all the work, digging us out of the mud after we hit the dead end that wasn't there before. *She* just tried to tell me what to do. Look at these hands. I broke two fingernails."

"Huh!" said Maddy, tossing her long mane of jet black hair. My heart misfired. "I would have helped, but you only had one shovel."

"So you had to bash my shovel's handle with a rock and just about pulp my hand in the process," Victoria interrupted. She paused and regarded my worksheets that now littered the courtyard. "Are we having fun yet?"

"Travis and Damien are having fun," I observed glumly.

"Where are they?"

"Ask me something I know."

"If they're not here," said Victoria, "they miss tea and too bloody bad."

"First things first," said Maddy. "Do we have a replacement for Steve?"

Victoria read my resigned sigh perfectly. "Why am I not surprised?"

"OK, nothing we can do about that," Maddy continued. "We have to organise these kids, get them to tidy this mess and alert school about Damien and Travis. Have you got reception on your phone, Peter?"

"Not yet," I lamented. "You?"

"No."

"That makes three of us," added Victoria.

"Where are the Camp staff?" Maddy demanded, her violet eyes holding me in her divine power. I shrugged helplessly.

Turning the master switch back on in the fuse box at least gave us lights. The office was locked and devoid of life. The only phone that might work sat on the front desk behind it.

By the time Tony and Doc arrived, Victoria and Maddy had managed to evict the boys from the girls' dorm. Next, Tony and I had to remove the girls from the boys' dorm. Doc coordinated a litter patrol before dinner was served.

Blake and Tristan threw the remaining worksheets into the campfire. Next, we had to prevent the fire spreading, when wind gusted the flaming paperwork and set it randomly in and among the bush nearby. Finally, we utilised the promise of hot food and the oncoming darkness to restrict students to gaming on their phones in the dorms. Enforced Facebook denial meant one less way to bully each other.

We barbecued sausages, onion and potatoes and served them with bread and tomato sauce, accompanied by apple juice and raspberry cordial. No camp staff appeared. Steve's replacement remained a theoretical entity.

Damien and Travis remained at large.

Monday, 8.30 p.m.

"Let the cold and dark bring them to us," Doc decided, gazing into the gloom as we sat around the fire.

"But what if something happens to them?" Maddy agonised.

"The Devil looks after his own," said Doc. "They'll be all right."

"They are not supposed to be here," Victoria rationalised. "They're suspended. They're not on our list. We can't be held responsible."

"We're stuck with them nevertheless," said Tony. "Can you imagine what our Duty of Care breach will look like if this shit hits the fan?"

"Not to forget the media," Doc added, editorialising: "Boys perish in thick scrub. Negligent teachers to blame."

"No such thing as a bad student..." Tony opined ironically.

"Can't be the parents' fault," Doc smirked.

Maddy frowned.

"There's only one solution," said Doc, producing a two-litre apple juice bottle from his pack. "Pass me your cups."

Maddy spluttered, when the Johnnie Walker met her palate.

"I thought you were joking when you mentioned this," I said, accepting a generous splash. "But you're right. Apple juice is the same colour –"

"Loose lips sink ships, Peter," Tony interrupted, shooting me a warning glance. "Thanks, Doc."

"You can thank me in your eulogy at my funeral."

Doc first made that remark the day after his doctor advised him to retire from teaching. The occasion was a particularly tedious staff meeting: forty minutes of Ferrier droning about the importance of punctuality to class and yard duty and its connection with professional wellness, followed by Naomi's nasal offerings on a more structured, but student-interest-centred Pastoral Care. Doc renamed it in undertones as Pastoral Waste of Time. I laughed out loud, sealing my doom in Naomi's eyes. Doc's demise had long since been sealed.

Doc re-filled Tony's mug and mine. Maddy placed a declining hand across hers and stood.

"We have to do something about Damien and Travis!" she insisted.

"I know what I would have liked to do to Travis last year –" I began, as the whisky coursed through my head.

"Don't," Maddy said briefly. Our eyes met. "I'm going to look for them."

"I'm coming with you."

I tossed back the liquor and hurried through the boys' dorm to the separate room where Tony, Doc and I had bunks, covertly checking faces in case Travis and Damien had crept back. The boys were mostly immersed in phones or iPods.

"Can we come?" asked Blake.

"No."

"Why?"

"It's not safe."

"It's not fair," Blake complained. "Travis is my friend."

"He could be dead," Trent shouted. Numerous voices chimed in.

"I'm comin' to look for him," said Blake, pulling on his hoodie.

"No!"

"No!" repeated Tony, firmly blocking the door. "No one is to leave. You heard Mr Moon. It isn't safe." Rebellion wavered, then subsided.

Maddy emerged from the female dorm. At the edge of the clearing our torch beams lit the path in the thick scrub that surrounded the building. In the darkness my heart pounded at her subtle fragrance and the tiny sound of her breathing. Our footfalls crunched in the night silence.

"Are you OK?" she whispered.

"No… I mean, yes…"

Maddy shone her torch into my face. "Are you sure?"

"Nothing another apple juice won't cure." My attempted reassuring smile stalled her further dissection of my naked desire.

I checked my phone and to my surprise it showed a signal. Having long since retained Mrs Armour's number, I dialled it, but got the usual recorded invitation: leave a message to be converted into a ten-second text. There's only so much bad news a teacher can wedge into ten seconds.

"Hello? Mrs Armour? This is Peter Moon from Happy Vale High School. I'm calling from Year Nine Camp, where your son has come without permission, and –"

"At least you got through," said Maddy quietly. "My phone is still dead."

"What do you say to Mrs Armour, anyway?" I mused out loud, unable to contain myself. "What *can* you say?"

"The truth," Maddy responded. "Travis has made a bad choice –"

"– another bad choice –"

"And we need to alert her as is required by our Duty of Care."

"He's not supposed to be here."

"But he *is* here. Peter, we are responsible."

"Isn't Mrs Armour responsible? She let him come."

"Peter, you know that isn't likely."

"And yet he is here. We need to find him and Damien and get them the hell out of here –"

"Back on the street where they will go? Aren't they better off here?"

"It doesn't help us."

"Peter, why do you see the down side of those boys being here? Why not see this as an opportunity?"

A dull feeling of inadequacy swept through me. Again, my anger at the world foisting Travis Armour in my face was setting me at odds with the object of my heart's fondest desire. I realised she wanted an answer.

"Opportunity?"

"It's a chance to work with Travis away from his home environment. He's here with us 24-7. We can help him see another way to behave, to live."

"Maddy, with all due respect, even if we found him now and steered him back to camp, we only have a few days to undo fourteen years of what you call 'under-parenting' and what I call criminal neglect –"

"Peter," she sighed. The music in her voice sang to my soul. But her words cut to the essence of my dilemma, my five years of dread as to whether this career was one massive mistake, or whether I was put here by some droll sense of divine comedy to suffer for love. "We *can* make a difference. We *have* it in us to change the world. We've taken this path and have the precious charge of the lives in our care. While we're on this path, while these kids are our 24-7 responsibility, it is our *duty* to make every second count."

"Mrs Armour had Travis when she was a drugged-up seventeen-year-old," I protested, "and his dad is never out of jail long enough for Travis to know his face. It seems to me we have no chance."

"Peter," she admonished, musically but humiliatingly. "We have no *choice*. Travis may have been disadvantaged, but his choices are *not* pre-determined, as you seem to be saying –"

Suddenly Maddy gasped and fell to the ground.

"Maddy!"

"Ouch," she breathed. "My ankle. I've twisted it. Ouch!"

I helped her to her feet, shamelessly holding her in my arms and breathing in the magic of her closeness.

"Lean on me," I offered with one or two passing ironic thoughts as to my opportunism. "I'll get you back to camp."

"We should keep looking," she protested. "My ankle's...not too bad...ouch!"

With me supporting her probably more than what was necessary, we hobbled along the path for a half an hour, pausing frequently, but nothing disturbed the deep silence of the bush. Returning to camp, our footfalls were the only sound for kilometres around. My phone stayed silent.

"Damien and Travis are still with the other feral animals, it seems," Doc mused, as we re-entered the campfire's glow. There was discernible glow in the faces of our three colleagues as well. The breathless silence remained. Victoria leapt to help Maddy when she saw her problem. In a moment Maddy was in a chair with her ankle elevated, ice packs rendered useless by the unavailability of refrigeration.

"It's almost too quiet," Victoria commented as she sat next to Maddy.

"They've gone to ground," Tony muttered.

"Damien and Travis are upholding the honour of Happy Vale," Doc added with mock solemnity. "Our younger colleagues must appreciate that, over twenty years, Happy Vale's leading alumni *have* gone to ground: a gangland boss, a phalanx of his minions, convicted murderers, copious sex offenders, welfare opportunists, hookers, junkies, busted drug dealers, con men, house-breakers, serially unemployed and terminally unemployable."

"So, Doc," Victoria dead-panned. "Your pedagogy is working."

"I automatically inspire," Doc declaimed, nodding infinitesimally to Victoria, "thirty differing intellectual, spiritual and physical beings with brilliantly engaging curriculum that unfailingly zeroes into the parameters of their collective and separate interests. I juggle daily learning tasks for readers of chunky vampire trilogies with those who can't read."

Laughter drew curious glances from both dorms.

"Bed!" Tony ordered.

"Gaming extravaganzas have nothing on my classes," Tony smirked, accepting another shot.

"I am empowered," Doc continued, "to equate - in earnest consultation with the children, you understand - a love of words and knowledge with a superficial, glamorous cyber-universe of non-stop virtual excitement. I do it all day, every day."

Tony wheezed with suppressed laughter. Victoria smiled. Doc poured another round with a shaking hand. Maddy glared at her unresponsive phone and shook her head in bemused wonder.

"What do you really do in your classes?" she probed.

"Year Nine English is a circus," Doc offered. "Drama lurches from farce to tragedy."

"Peter's Year Twelve play was *good*," Maddy protested. She turned to me, eyes flashing, full lips parted heart-stoppingly. "No, really. Getting those guys to do Shakespeare was amazing."

The fullness of her attention sucked the air from my lungs, precluding any self-effacing display of modesty. Instead, I beamed like a six-year-old. I saw Tony's feline, knowing grin in response. He knew the play wasn't Shakespeare.

"Maddy," Tony responded. "The Year Twelve play makes the newsletter because it's good. The antics of Pete's Year Eights and Nines do not. You know why."

"I spend a lot of teaching time guarding the cut-out switches in the lab," said Victoria. "If the switches are disabled, you can't cut the gas. And the apprentice pyromaniacs love playing with them. Of course, fires break out in your classroom when lit Bunsen burners come into contact with dried-out fabric on twenty-year-old notice boards. Remember my lab fire?"

"I remember how the forms for that disappeared as well," Doc said.

"If my senior Business Studies class is before recess," Tony bemoaned, "it can be pretty quiet. Most need their beauty sleep until ten."

"I must lead a sheltered life," Maddy mused. "In my class we do Music. It's not always easy –"

"Don't get me wrong, Maddy," Victoria cut in, "but don't forget the state-of-the-art Music facilities they made sure you had. Graham knew you were a gem the moment he laid eyes on you. No effort was spared for you."

"She's right, Maddy," added Tony.

"What about you guys?" Maddy asked. "Really?"

"You've seen Hell Alley," said Doc. "Smashed up, tagged portable classrooms. Air conditioning breaks down, no internet access."

"I never went there at all," said Maddy, "until this year, when I got a couple of relief lessons down there."

"Yes," said Doc, "they truly looked after you."

"It's like this, Maddy," Tony explained. "We have to lower our expectations to base level. Most kids think they can do whatever they like in mainstream classes. For your own sanity, you have to keep them busy."

"What do you do?" asked Maddy.

"Copy from the board," said Tony. "No one goes until they're finished."

"That's it?"

"That's a fair bit of it. You can tell them to copy from books, although that often leads to vandalism and graffiti in the books."

"Old-fashioned, teacher-directed instruction is in vogue in the trenches," Doc added. "Show me a New Age Affirmative Educator who gets Travis, Damien, Trent and co to wrap their grey matter around the curriculum and I'll show you an old-fashioned bullshit artist. Or a miracle worker."

"Nevertheless," Tony added, "we know that some kids sense school is more than a place to meet your friends and socialise –"

"However unlikely that might seem," Doc smirked.

"That's not fair, Doc." Maddy was genuinely indignant.

"Somehow, copying notes counts as education," Tony continued. "It provides them and their parents with evidence that learning is occurring. It's the kind of classroom experience many parents remember. Strangely, most kids will copy from the board, if you don't expect much else from them."

"And if you don't expect them to copy too much," added Victoria.

"OK, what is too much writing in one lesson?" Maddy asked.

"More than half a page," said Tony.

"Only a hundred or so words? In three quarters of an hour?"

"My Nines last year might do half a page on a good day," Doc lamented. "Don't forget that the first five to fifteen minutes are needed to settle the class and the last ten are about preventing them leaving early."

"Then there are the kids who can't write," said Tony.

Maddy shook her head in quiet dismay.

"All this Affirmative Ed stuff is fine in theory," Victoria griped, "but it assumes that kids are in state-of-the-art classrooms with all the bells and whistles, free of habitual trouble-makers."

"It also makes the extraordinary assumption," Doc added, "that it can operate without an effective Behaviour Management system with real consequences that deter disruptive behaviour."

There was a silence that began to stretch.

"You've been a teacher for a long time, Tony," Maddy stated. "What keeps you going?"

"My retirement plan of a small business consultancy," he replied. "It's still a way off, but I do like showing kids what a bit of enterprise can get them. Now and then someone picks up the ball and runs with it."

"Tony," Doc admonished. "You're too modest by half." To Maddy, he added: "The man is a master."

"No doubt," Maddy smiled. "What about you, Doc? What keeps you going?"

"The knowledge that I still don't have enough in my superannuation fund," Doc answered in a matter-of-fact way. Then his warped grin flashed. "Let me tell you something. A long time ago, there was a young boy in a big class in a run-down primary school in a poor suburb. He sat passively and watched the other boys get the strap or the cane for the most minor infractions. His mind wandered when the old teacher delivered the never-ending lectures on subjects long since consigned to the dustbin of history and wondered how long it would be before he would be set free. Then, one day, the old teacher failed to appear and another - younger - man, took his place. From that day on, the boy saw the world anew. Instead it was a place of limitless possibility, of limitless opportunity. Why? Because that young teacher had within him the divine capacity to inspire the love of learning. The young boy had found his mentor and the way to freedom."

"Nice story, Doc," said Maddy. "All true?"

"All true."

"And –?"

"It keeps me going," Doc admitted.

"I knew there was more to it than apple juice," Tony observed.

"You know," Doc added, "every now and then I get a little reminder of what it felt like. Occasionally, just often enough, something good happens in my class. There's a light bulb moment. Some kid or other, often the most unlikely...*gets* it. Different every time, but the same feeling. The truth will set that kid free. I teach for that moment, for it is in that moment I *am* that young man with the divine spark and I *can* move mountains."

"Thanks for telling us that," Maddy whispered.

"That moment makes it possible to forgive almost any transgression," Doc concluded.

In the silence that followed, Victoria tried her phone and sighed.

"I haven't heard from Travis Armour's mother," I noted. "My signal's gone again anyway."

"Mrs Armour is one for whom that moment of truth has definitely not occurred," said Doc, imbibing again. "I taught her, you know. If teaching is a word one could use for our interactions."

"I'm guessing she was away a lot," I mused, "if her son's attendance record and number of suspensions are any indication."

"Speaking of the habitually absent," Doc continued, easing away from such rare self-disclosure, "Elspeth was missing again last Friday. I had the pleasure of her Year Eight Drama class, a Dreamtime role-play as spirits of the Rainbow Serpent in primal one-ness with the land, then for homework a journal entry encapsulating that bond with Mother Earth."

"You didn't do that, did you?" Tony spluttered.

"Of course not. I had a Mr Bean DVD. Our colleague here, Mr Moon, through his studied classroom management has ensured that the TV and teacher's chair in Drama One have not yet been destroyed." Doc flashed an ironic grin. "My poor, put-upon posterior thanks you, young sir."

"Security was down when Doc tried to sit on his chair," Tony clarified.

"Vegemite on the security camera lens that time," Doc recounted dryly.

"Doc's classes were moved to a portable in Hell Alley," Tony continued. "The room he was using needed an upgrade to become Sam's swish new office."

"This was, of course," Doc added, "when he secured the plum: Director of Affirmative Education. When that office became available, the myth existed that applications might be open to the most appropriate candidate."

"That's assuming all potential candidates were aware of its availability," Victoria commented knowingly.

"Yes," Doc concurred. "Did you see the advert, Maddy?"

"No," she replied. "I'll admit I did not."

"It went up at 4.57 on a Friday, with an application deadline of 9.30 the following Monday. Only the most efficient operator could be considered."

"Yes," Tony smirked. "It helped that the operator in question was the only one aware of the ad's existence."

I laughed again. Tony quivered with mirth. Victoria snorted and shook silently, but Maddy remained unmoved.

"And then there was the other myth," Doc confided, "that centred on the office being in any way useful to the troops down in Hell Alley. The kiddies suffered a downturn in their wellness down in Purgatory."

"None of them had parents on Council," Tony noted. "That's for sure."

"The poor delicate young creatures objected to not having the comforts of functional air conditioning," Doc drawled. "Somehow it was my fault. To cut a long story short, Chad Robertson pulled the chair out from where I was going to sit, causing me to land inelegantly on my arse, undo two years of costly chiropractic therapy and bring on my second heart attack."

"What?" Maddy was incredulous. "I never knew that."

"Doc had a term off," said Tony, his grin cat-like. "Don't you recall?"

"No," said Maddy. "I don't."

"It devoured my sick leave," Doc added, "until WorkCare finally approved my claim. Ferrier dealt with it, so it goes without saying that nothing happened. The boy denied everything and Ferrier backed him. They couldn't see anything on the surveillance monitors. Our esteemed leader, Mr Ferrier, emulating his predecessor, the almighty Graham Fleming, places such trust in the innate truthfulness of the cherubs. My ongoing health is but a small price to pay. It cost me close to a year's salary and twice that in recovery time."

Maddy stared incredulously. "How many others –?"

"Plenty," said Tony.

"Good example," Doc corroborated, "when Brendan Wagner kicked Vince Sorrento in the ribs. We had the constabulary in for that."

"I remember Vince," Maddy gasped, "but I don't remember –"

"Apparently Mr Sorrento had told Brendan for the third time to turn the ghetto blaster off and put it back in the storeroom from whence he pinched it," said Doc. "Young Brendan felt that some ear-shattering rap would be a welcome addition, as Mr Sorrento's boring voice directing the Year Ten class play did not allow for sufficient student input to the curriculum."

"I would have put it back myself and locked the storeroom," I said.

"The same thought occurred to Vince," Doc sighed. "Sadly, he chose not to negotiate with Brendan for a win-win outcome. Brendan disagreed, which led to the unfortunate accident."

"Accident?" Maddy queried. "You said Brendan kicked him."

"Oh, yes," Tony added. "Brendan assured Naomi it was an accident."

"He slipped," Doc continued, "when Mr Sorrento was ordering him around and trying to tear the handle of the ghetto blaster out of his hands. As you know, Mademoiselle Madeleine, 'accidents' can and do happen."

Doc traced an imaginary scar on his well-worn visage. Maddy frowned, but nodded almost imperceptibly.

"What happened to Brendan?"

"Oh, he was counselled within an inch of his life," said Doc. "Naomi helped him understand that while loud rap music had its place, it was on this occasion not the edge the Drama rehearsal needed for its success."

"What about the police?" Maddy demanded.

"They were there to investigate the charge made by Brendan's mother that Vince Sorrento assaulted her son," said Tony.

Maddy gasped. "Why didn't he go to the Union?"

"Two reasons," said Victoria. "One: Vince had resigned from the Union in protest, because the dues he had paid had not resulted in any help with his concerns. And two: Mary, the Union Rep at the time, was on sick leave herself. WorkCare came good for Doc a year later with a lump sum."

"Too little too late," Doc opined, "but better than nothing."

"Tell her why Vince didn't have Brendan charged," Tony urged.

"He was told not to," Doc explained. "He made the first aggressive move by trying to take the ghetto blaster off the kid."

"He wasn't allowed near the office when the police and the mother were there," Tony added. "Graham smoothed it all over, as always."

"What about Vince's ribs?" she asked incredulously.

"Cracked, but covered by insurance," Doc answered.

"We didn't see much of Vince after that," said Victoria. "Last we heard he was training to enter the Ministry. Elspeth replaced him."

"Elspeth is a protected species," I observed.

Tony smirked, Victoria nodded, but Maddy frowned.

"Peter," Maddy admonished. "That's not fair."

"If Elspeth has any more unexplained days off," Doc scoffed, "she could die, be kept at the back of the Home Economics freezer, her body used for cryogenic research, and still collect her fortnightly pay. I'd say it was fair."

It was Doc's oblique way of referring to the little-known event of Elspeth's meltdown at a previous school. Under Graham's watch she was the counsellor who cared too much, the Drama teacher who burnt out trying to go places few, if any, adolescents cared to go. As always Doc knew someone who knew someone who whispered juicy details of Elspeth's hospitalisation.

Graham, her line manager, had taken his eyes off the ball. It was a lesson for him. Elspeth's rehab became his business, her painless re-entry to work in Graham's new domain translated to half-time work for full-time pay that included a portfolio without substance: arts advisory coordinator. After Graham vanished, so did any pretence that the position meant anything.

Maddy shook her head at her phone, switched it off and stood.

"I'm going to bed," she announced.

Victoria rose and began helping her to the dorm.

"We should all go," said Tony. "I'll get up early and see if I can find any sign of Travis and Damien."

Tuesday, 7.30 a.m.

.

"Remember the Healthy Eating Policy?" Doc mused though a mouthful of bacon, as fat splattered from the barbecue breakfast.

"Before my time," I mumbled through my encore hangover.

"It was a document rivalled in length by *War and Peace* and the *Old Testament*," Doc pronounced, "lacking the literary merit of the former and the spiritual significance of the latter. You, sir, have infringed every tenet of its egregious exhortation. Well done."

Doc helped himself to another generous rasher, wrapped it in bread and filled the kettle with rainwater. The first of our charges began appearing and I knew without looking that Maddy was limping to the barbecue area. Her subtle fragrance floated above the succulent bacon. Victoria hurried to Maddy and helped her to a chair.

"How is it this morning?" she asked.

"I'll live," Maddy replied quietly.

"You'll have to keep it up this morning," Victoria continued, concerned. "It's still swollen."

I inhaled deeply and pondered yet again the imponderable differences between Maddy and me. Despite consistently going the extra mile to make my Drama classes work and make my productions succeed, could I find that extra something that Maddy invariably did? Despite my library of alternate learning plans, my reams of illustrated, annotated worksheets for the work-shy, my lesson plans burnished to user-friendly polish in the furnace of Year Nine English and despite the thickness of my hide that had been tanned to leathery near-imperviousness through repeated floggings by the recalcitrant, could I ever rise to her saintly practicality and unflappable coolness?

Would I ever be able to achieve that unaccountable serenity, that divine patience and goodwill, that immense generosity that enabled her to bring any child into her universe, no matter how inherently appalling? Could I make myself worthy of her? Could I actually forgive Travis?

"Agenda from the first Affirmative Ed staff meeting," announced Victoria. "Conditions under which an unscheduled full staff meeting could be scheduled: I reckon we have them here. It's over twelve hours since we last saw two students in our care –"

"Agenda Item Number One," Doc intoned, "crucifixion of irresponsible educators driving innocent youngsters into wilderness."

Tony appeared from the track that led into the bush.

"I looked all around since first light," he said. "Nothing."

"Seriously," Victoria interposed. "What are we going to do? If they do re-appear miraculously, we have no choice other than to accept them into the fold. And that's just one crisis averted. Where's our support? How we are going to manage the canoeing, the horse-riding and the abseiling?"

"Activities parents have shelled out money for," Tony observed.

"I have never dangled by rope off the edge of a cliff," Doc muttered, before swallowing two small tablets with water. "And I'm not starting now."

"If we haven't got the professionals here to supervise," I suggested, as I turned the pile of bacon, rasher by rasher, "then we will have to tell the finance office to refund parents."

"Charity will love that," Doc observed drily.

"She'll have no choice," Victoria noted.

"Charity Lovejoy is driven by three urges," Doc added: "love of purse-string control, loyalty to Naomi and Ron and hatred of Tony and me."

"I get the first two," said Maddy, rubbing her ankle gingerly and wincing in obvious discomfort, "but not the last."

"We exposed her corruption," said Tony.

"Charity? Corrupt?"

"Missing pavers and decking materials from the school upgrade," said Doc, "materialised around Graham's pool."

"Remember the odd-job man, who helped out down at Tech Studies? We called him the Rat," said Tony. Maddy nodded, wide-eyed. "Rambo caught him out, pilfering some of the timber meant for woodwork. He wondered why the timber always came at seven a.m. on a Monday. The order forms were done by someone who wanted pine for off-site building projects."

"And that same person accidentally ordered far too many pavers for the upgrade of the central courtyard," said Doc.

"Graham enlisted the Rat," Tony continued. "He became a source of free labour and materials at Graham's five-acre hacienda out there at the Paradise end of Happy Vale."

"He had the receipts detailing massive pilfering on the Rat's part," Doc added. "For Graham to keep quiet, the Rat found himself obliged to perform extra duties at the hacienda, building a gazebo, a wine cellar, a massive veranda extension and laying the surplus pavers. Since we've been a Local Responsibility school, our leaders administer finances as they see fit."

"I find it hard to accept all that," Maddy breathed.

"It's straight out theft," Doc added. "Believe it or not, it's true."

"The Rat's cousin has trade contacts," said Tony.

"The Rat did all that work at Graham's?" I asked, imagining him slaving early morning and late at night for weeks, punishment for being caught.

"No," Doc said, tones hardening. "Ron Ferrier, and others, plus spouses, spent a few Sundays out there, labouring for love of their Principal, catered by the wonderful Kathy Lloyd, whose gourmet cuisine was matched only by the fine wines served."

"We started keeping a diary," said Tony.

"A little record," Doc added, "of some of the more unorthodox methodologies employed at Happy Vale, if we're ever required to give evidence in the future. It's kept me amused, especially while we are forced to listen in staff meetings to hot air coming from all points North of our position."

"Love those hot Northerlies," Victoria smirked.

"We can't touch Graham now," said Tony. "We only have anecdotal evidence about the pilfering. Virtually no one else knows anything about it."

"The way the committees are stacked at Happy Vale, no one in positions ironically deemed 'responsible' would ever tell a court of law that everything was anything less than wonderful," Doc added.

"Of course," Maddy whispered. She switched her phone on and stared intently as it came to life. "I remember thinking I had seen those pavers somewhere, one time at Graham's for Sunday lunch."

"When you were in the 'In' crowd," Victoria breathed.

Maddy sighed. "Yes, I was innocent. How did Charity keep her job?"

After repeated painful exchanges with Charity over imperfect theatre excursion paperwork and Drama budget blowouts, I was interested as well.

"How doth the little crocodile," Doc warbled, "improve her shining tail?"

"Graham looked after his people very well," said Tony. "He produced paperwork that showed work on his property done independent of any school project. They were all in the clear, even though we saw Ron and his henchmen load the pavers onto a trailer behind the car being driven by Graham. The lawyers backed off. But that was the end of any chance Doc and I had of a fair deal from Admin on anything we wanted."

"We've been bad-mouthed behind closed doors," said Doc, "Shafted with the long handle. No promotion, no transfer, no recourse. No other school in the region will touch us. It appears that Miss Meredith and Mr Ferrier have learnt well from the master. They'll squirm out of anything, like sending us on this camp without Steve."

"The conference is far too important to them," Tony added. "Whatever comes of this will go on the backburner. Isn't that right, Maddy?"

"A year ago I'd have been at your throat over that," Maddy observed evenly. She exhaled, annoyance clouding her loveliness. "Still no signal."

"A year ago you were still their princess," Victoria smirked.

"You're not wrong," Maddy conceded, touching her scar. "I'm marked for life. I look at Travis Armour and know he is a damaged boy and maybe I can help him, but … it's hard now, harder than before."

"Hence Plan B?" Victoria commented archly.

"I once thought I'd make my whole career at Happy Vale," Maddy fretted. "But now –"

48

"The joy of innocence," Doc murmured. "In the meantime –"

"How are we going to keep the kids occupied?" Victoria concluded.

"Somehow," said Maddy. She began looking through the paperwork in her shoulder bag. "We'll think of something. We have to."

Lifting eggs and bacon clear of the hotplate, I drank in Maddy's morning light radiance, lost again in the magical dream of basking in her love.

"Affirmative Education is theoretically about teaching renewal of spirit," Doc declaimed. Without undue irony, he added: "Maddy, you are an inspiration to us all."

"Thank God for Maddy," said Victoria. "School's a disaster, kids run riot and Admin ignores the problem. Put on the blinkers, perform basic duties, attempt a smile of Wellness and tick off the days 'til retirement."

"Last time I looked," I essayed, "I had just thirteen thousand days left."

The others chuckled, but Maddy remained unmoved.

"Guys," she sighed. "We need to alert the authorities about Damien and Travis. We have to go back to the nearest town and call school."

"And tell them we've lost Damien and Travis?" I queried.

"You mean," Doc interrupted, "tell them their negligence allowed two suspended students to stow away. Of course, our esteemed Miss Meredith will hold young Peter Moon accountable for this regrettable lapse, he being the teacher with Duty of Care."

"Thanks for that, Doc," I dead-panned.

"Happy to help," he intoned.

"You're right, Maddy," said Tony. "We can't just hope they come back."

"Give me a bacon sandwich and coffee," said Victoria. "I'll eat as I go."

The kids were spilling from the dorms and we turned our attention to feeding them. Victoria discreetly withdrew and went to her car, which she had parked in the small car park behind the main building. White-faced and trembling, she returned a moment later and beckoned with her eyes. Tony and I joined her to one side of the noisily feeding throng.

"I'm not going anywhere," she whispered. "My tyres are slashed."

"It's over fifty kilometres to the nearest town," said Tony. He looked at me. "How's your long distance running?"

"What?" I felt the blood drain from my cheeks.

"I'm afraid so," said Tony. "You're the one likely to do it the quickest."

"What about those women from yesterday?"

"Gone," said Tony. "I thought of them when I first went out, but they must have left last night. There's no trace of them, or anyone else."

We re-joined Doc and Maddy and acquainted them with the latest challenge to our collective wellness.

"We have to keep the kids busy," Maddy exclaimed, unfolding some of the papers she had in her shoulder bag. "We can start them on the bush trails, following this map, calculating the distance walked and identifying flora and fauna. I can get that started."

"I'll do that," said Tony.

Doc seethed, his eyes shut as if in pain.

"I knew I should have got it in writing from the quack that I was unfit for this," he lamented. "All right. I'll come."

There was a long moment of silence.

"No, Doc," said Maddy. "I'll go. We need someone here if anyone turns up."

"Maddy," Victoria admonished, "you are not going anywhere on that ankle. I'll go with Tony."

"Two of you with ninety-seven kids?" Doc objected. "Dicky ticker or no, I'm in as well. Mademoiselle, you get to sit this one out. I, er, *we* need that ankle operational again."

Maddy smiled. My heart did a double backflip.

"I'm already stressed about my car," Victoria announced. "I need to keep occupied. Let's get started."

Several of the girls hurtled towards us, Karen and Sarah in their midst.

"Miss Green?" cried Karen. "Your car tyres are all flat."

Several of the boys hurried off to gawk at the damage, returning to the hubbub of many teenage voices. In seconds the entire student body was present.

51

Our stranding evoked every kind of reaction. Emotions threatened to boil over into uncontrollable chaos.

"Quiet!" Tony bellowed. He stood on an outdoor bench. "Pay attention."

The volume dipped a few points.

"Listen to Mr Amadio," Maddy commanded, her ringing tones raising the hairs on my arms and the back of my neck.

The kids saw her steely expression, the white scar jagging across her heart-shaped face, the determined thrust of her jaw, her hair billowing in the breeze. The scar added to her mystique. Suffering had made her more powerful. I ached for her.

The clamour receded to nothing in a heart-beat.

"Getting upset isn't going to help," Tony pronounced. "We all need to settle down. Put aside what we can't control and focus on things we can manage. We have a program of activities that are linked to the curriculum. I am sure that we'll get on just fine if we all work together. Don't forget, we are still in school here –"

"Fuck school!" Blake sneered.

"Blake," said Maddy, suddenly in his face. "I have spoken to you before about this. Remember our conversation with your grandma last year?"

Blake flushed. Imminent rebellion expired.

"Sorry," he mumbled.

"You made a promise to me, Blake," Maddy warned him in silken tones. "Now, are you going to behave?"

52

"I guess," Blake muttered from the depths of his untidy fringe and the peak of his baseball cap. The silence was absolute. His humiliation complete, Blake met my eyes with unqualified malevolence.

"Anyone else have a problem?" Tony challenged. The silence stretched and strained. "OK, in twenty minutes we are beginning the first orienteering exercise. We'll divide you into three groups and give the instructions then. In the meantime, you have free time to finish eating, have a drink and to get ready for some bush-walking. Annika, you can't wear those."

Already the $9.99 pink Ugg boots were scuffed and worn-looking.

"But I haven't got anything else," she whined.

"I'll try to find you something," said Maddy.

"But these are comfortable," Annika protested.

"You won't be comfortable on a bush track," Doc observed, "when they fall apart after twenty minutes."

"I don't want to go," Annika whined. "What's the point? Why can't we just stay here and relax?"

"You can be the reporter for your group," said Maddy crisply. "I will want to hear your report later today."

Doc selected three groups with an even compliant to trouble-maker spread in each. Name lists were hastily prepared. Blake, Trent and Tristan were separated. Tony enforced the separation and led the group with Blake off into the bush.

Tuesday, 9.00 a.m.

"Peter," said Maddy. "Are you going to be OK?"

"Sure," I lied, drinking her music, living in hope. Could that concern in her eyes and voice mean more? A marathon completed at uni was a distant enough memory for me to recall the fierce joy of finishing but not the pain.

"Take plenty of water," said Victoria, thrusting a full drink bottle into my backpack. "And a jumper. It will get cold when you stop for a rest. Good luck." She hurried off to lead her group down a different track to the one Tony took.

"Have my bottle as well," said Doc. He offered a lop-sided grin. "No, it only has water in it."

"You'd better take something to eat," added Maddy. She cut some bacon and tomato sandwiches.

"Make sure you have change for a public phone," said Doc. He thrust coins into my hand. I added them to the small change in my pocket.

I adjusted the straps of my backpack. Maddy and Doc gazed at me intently. A chilly breeze whipped through the thin fabric of my T-shirt.

"Well." The intimidating prospect of the open road swam before my eyes. "I suppose I'll be off."

"Try to flag someone down," Doc urged. "Remember, you're doing this because of our Duty of Care. Your priority is to get the necessary messages to school that the wellness of our students is at risk. The thicker you lay that on, the more they'll listen."

"Good luck, Peter." Maddy smiled. Angels sang.

I would be lucky to get to the nearest town before lunch-time. The forest continued to stifle phone signals. I marvelled again at how simple choices steered lives. My marks had been good enough for law, but I could make more of a difference being a teacher, an influential voice in a reputable educational institution.

I made many assumptions in those days, the most fanciful, it seemed, being the one about having an influence. And yet, I told myself, remember Doc's words on the divine spark and the moments that mattered. And look at what influence Maddy had. Was it in her from birth? Or did she learn that magic that wrapped the teens around her little finger? Was it some kind of celestial club for the inspired? Once in, could my pedagogy and my pronouncements change lives and make kids believe? Could I take that extra leap into the infinite well-spring of love, from whence my fingertips would spread the gold dust that ensured my legend at Happy Vale?

The words 'Happy Vale' conjured instant images of Ferrier and Naomi and the dream evaporated. Once upon a time, Doc was fond of reminding us, a gathering of teaching colleagues in the staff room meant an exchange of information between the principal and the staff, laced with liberal two-way conversation and consultation. Teachers could frame motions, speak to them, were empowered to put the motions to vote and in so doing had an active say in framing the school's policies and modes of operation. Once we were an inter-active assembly of professionals sharing equal rights to speak and be heard. Not any more: now we got talked at. We might speak only when invited to brainstorm during so-called training and development.

My mind drifted to the latest unscheduled Wellness presentation. It had caused Doc to miss his medical appointment. The presenter, an authority in her field, had emailed to say that she had two free hours after all and could accept our offer to speak. Sam fell into a lather of excitement. The opportunity was a steal, at just four hundred bucks an hour. The email to all staff required our attendance. As an added joy, we could add the hours to our mandatory training and development time.

Lives went on hold. Prior appointments were cancelled. Marking and lesson preparation would replace family interaction. Parents of small children made hasty calls to extend after school care arrangements. Doc was delighted to remind us at lunch that our personal lives were so meaningless that we could dedicate our dead time to finding meaning and applying it to our pedagogy. Doc was denying himself further medication in the interests of higher learning.

"Just think," he drawled as the bell for Lesson Six shrilled. "You can entertain and instruct your families on the elasticity of the nerve endings in the cranial cavity and their capacity to flourish when the appropriate amount of niceness is inserted. It's a win-win."

The guest presenter with her colourful out-sized spectacles was slightly disconcerted by the mirth from our corner, before she settled into her lengthy discourse on the hypothalamus, its function in the brain and our collective approach teaching and learning. As she defined it, "we, as teachers" imposed our own adult perspective on learning with minimal student collaboration. She had exalted the notion of student empowerment, enthusing over the exhilaration of enhancing a child's teachability, to bring on renewal of hope and learning energy, which resulted in affirmation. Empowerment, Exhilaration, Teachability, Renewal, Affirmation - five words that spelt Admin's new buzz-word EXTRA. Doc dozed through a lot of it. He wasn't the only one.

Thick marker pens squeaked on butcher's paper: empowering strategies, exhilaratory indicators, optimism, enthusiasm mapped numerically. Personal growth became a formula, but when Doc - that relic of an era in which democracy permitted free speech - offered his unsought hypothesis: not passing up work equals not passing, Ferrier frowned and Naomi glowered.

Data filled the shocked chasm opened by Doc's heresy. Our guest filled the interactive whiteboard with seamless methodologies to renew students and enhance their teachability. Affirmative education emerged. Sam declared it 'EXTRA-licious'. The 'In' crowd basked in the ambient wellness.

A tiny snore escaped from Doc's open mouth during a lull in proceedings. Naomi's self-righteous anger was palpable. Lips tight with disapproval, Naomi inquired of Doc's plans to empower his Year Nines. His eyes opened. He fixed Naomi with his most sardonic expression and fell into a trap of his own making:

"Five of the boys would listen to rap on their iPods. Another five would play games on their laptops, another five would talk loudly and simultaneously about the drugs they took on the weekend. Several of the girls would suddenly need to go to the toilet or visit friends in other classes for very compelling but un-named reasons."

"Hamish," Ferrier objected. "Spare us your negativity."

"Where is the learning? Where are the coordinated sequential stages of skill development?" Doc probed.

Naomi ignored the reference to academic rigour: "What is wrong with a Year Nine boy responding to the lyrics of a rap artist?"

"What's right with it? Am I to tolerate adolescent infatuation with barely comprehensible sociopaths glamorising a life of drugs, misogyny and crime?"

"Lose the cynicism, Hamish," Sam urged. "Embrace EXTRA."

"I have already. Extra students in over-crowded classes, extra stress, extra paperwork to administer the extra disciplinary concerns I have because of extra opportunities students are allowed to create extra mayhem."

"You will find personal renewal in EXTRA —"

Doc blew the raspberry that required him to deliver a Please Explain later, behind closed doors. In Ferrier's office he declared that he would take Year Nines on a camping trip rather than waste his time listening to any more from a person who used the word 'teachability' in a sentence and expected to be taken seriously. Victoria, accompanying him as his Union representative, concurred. Tony and I had avoided all camps for a couple of years. Suddenly, the four of us had found ourselves on the EXTRA-curricular Year Nine Camp, with Mr/Ms 'X', the replacement Outdoor Ed teacher, supposedly joining us.

Maddy filled the remaining staff place as Year Nine Coordinator, after a series of strained meetings with Ferrier and Charity over incomplete compensation for her 'accident', a scenario that never would have played out while she was Graham's Princess of Happy Vale. Her senior student choir was so well drilled that their conference performances were to be self-managed. Had Graham still been in the chair, Doc opined, Maddy might have been fast-tracked to a senior Admin role by now, while continuing to manage the cream of her well-trained musical acolytes. Ferrier, having been promoted by default, had a default position on most things: do nothing, then nothing can go wrong. Sam, as line manager for the Arts, would be pleased to take the credit for the choir's polish and flair.

On top of being newly crowned Affirmative Ed director, Sam was Arts manager, Sub School leader and Special Events coordinator. His one class, a Year Twelve Media Studies elective of ten, spent most of their time behind film cameras or in the editing suite. Sam was usually somewhere else even more salubrious, another who had learnt well from Graham, the master.

A moment later the highway came into view. Doc had stopped caring. Was that true for me? A number of our Happy Vale colleagues lacked sufficient wellness and security of tenure to care any more about unchecked disruptive behaviour and its time-consuming documentation that invariably vanished into the vortex. I thought of Maddy and told myself I cared.

Tuesday, 11.30 a.m.

Less than halfway, beyond exhaustion, plodding, lungs burning, stitch jabbing, no cars in the past thirty minutes, I asked myself again: did I care?

Harsh crow caws mocked me. Sweat stung my eyes. Blisters burst on my feet. Warm fluid joined blood in my socks. Jogging for two kilometres and walking one, gradually the distance melted. A rare car ignored my frantic signals. A farm utility turned off up a dirt track about fifty metres behind me.

Finally, an ancient truck pulled up.

"I'm goin' as far as town," he rumbled. "Any good t' yez?"

"Thanks, mate."

Faint with relief, I clambered aboard. The blocky, weathered rustic gave a gap-toothed, quizzical gaze. Gears rasped and we chugged forward.

"Break down, did yer?"

"Er, yeah."

That was true. Law and order had broken down at Happy Vale. I sat back and closed my eyes for several minutes, as the fatigue overtook me.

He jolted me from near sleep: "Been walkin' long?"

"Yes. I'm keen to get to town."

"Where's y' car?"

"It's…ah…back at the Outdoor Ed place."

His gaze jerked violently around towards me.

"You know them bludgers?" he demanded.

"No," I said, instinct demanding reticence. "I'm just staying there."

"You tell them from me. They still owe me money for the lamb."

"Pardon?"

"I sold them lamb last spring and they haven't coughed up yet."

"Hang on," I said. "It's not up to us to pay bills. The finance officer —"

"Teachers? Always whingin'," he rambled on, as if I hadn't spoken. "Why don't y' get a proper job? Then y'll have somethin' to whinge about."

"That's one way of looking at it," I observed carefully.

"It ain't rocket science," he growled. "Y' work nine to three and get eleven weeks off a year. And the kids don't learn nuthin'. Y' got it easy."

"You are entitled to your opinion," I said.

"If y' did your job right, y'd have nuthin' t'complain about."

"Whatever," I mumbled, muscles cooling, lactic acid beginning to burn.

We approached a shed and a few tumbledown shacks. The truck pulled to a halt, ancient brakes squealing.

"Here we are," said the farmer. "Town."

He descended from the cabin and lumbered towards the near shack.

"Thanks," I said to his retreating back.

My phone stayed dead. I stumbled back towards the open road.

Tuesday, 2.00 p.m.

A bell clanged tiredly at the dilapidated service station. The screen door slammed behind me. The unkempt proprietor shuffled to the counter and studied me through guarded slits for eyes, xenophobe to alien.

"Can I help you?" he asked. Or not.

"Yes," I said. "I'm a teacher, and –"

"Teacher?" He spat the word.

"Please," I continued. "I need to call my school as a matter of emergency. We're at the Outdoor Ed centre –"

"That place?" he growled. "Bloody thieves."

"What are you saying?"

"Those bastards've taken this whole town for a ride. They owe us money. Big money. Every trader in this town has bills outstanding."

"Who from?"

"The bludgers that opened the place. We thought it'd be good for the town, regular orders...money comin' in. But we seen none of it!"

"There was a camp here not long ago. Didn't anyone stop here?"

"Nobody stops here. This place is dying."

"Look," I implored. "We have a hundred kids there and no Camp staff."

"Gone, have they?"

"I told you. No one is there. We're on our own."

"Not surprised. They haven't been paid for three months."

"Three months? Do you know them?"

"One of 'em's me cousin. Said she was goin' north. Had a job lined up."

He stared. "If you want something, hurry up. I'm shuttin' for lunch."

"Hang on," I stalled. "I need some help –"

"Listen," he grated. "That camp ain't getting' no help from no one in this town. Not until we see some dollars."

"Please, I need a telephone at least. I have to call school."

"Sorry. Can't help."

"We're a teacher down. We can't do the planned activities –"

"Stiff shit, pal. Now, if you don't want to buy anything –"

"Is there a public phone I can use?"

"Down the other end of the main street."

I trudged down the single lane that snaked through the town. He was right. The town was dying. Paint peeled, old litter swirled like autumn leaves, street dogs barked at me, but no one emerged from any of the dingy dwellings. The pub looked deserted. One faded-looking supermarket was doing desultory trade. Eventually, the sole public phone came into view.

I dialled school. Normally, front office would answer after a few rings. This time it rang until the message kicked in. The line went dead before I had made our plight clear. My second attempt was cut off mid-sentence, as I was highlighting how our students were 'at risk of adverse wellness outcomes'.

That was direct from Doc's lexicon of bullshit for the desperate. I devoured my sandwiches and drank one water bottle in a single thirsty gulp. Surely someone would answer this time.

Dial tone preceded the disagreeably familiar: "Good afternoon. Happy Vale High School, home of Affirmative Education. Charity Lovejoy speaking."

"Charity. Peter Moon here. Listen, I need to speak to Naomi –"

"Naomi's not available. She's in a Plenary Session."

"It's important. Is Ron there?"

"He's in a meeting with the Minister. Can't be disturbed."

"Charity, this is an emergency –"

"Being a teacher down isn't an emergency. Calm down. Hasn't Steve's replacement turned up yet?"

"No. There is no replacement –"

"You don't know that!"

"Where is he then?"

"I don't know –"

"Has there even been an appointment?"

"I haven't got time for this," she snapped. "Just do what you have to!"

"Charity!" I protested. "You don't understand. I need to speak to Ron. Please get him out of that meeting."

"I'll thank you not to take that tone with me. Whatever your little problem is, it can wait."

"It's an emergency!" I implored. "We need –"

The phone cut out and my change was gone. My phone was still out of commission. The pub was my last chance.

The door creaked asthmatically and the heads of three elderly men at the bar turned as one on my entrance. I approached the bar under the silent basilisk stare of the trio. After a long moment, a sour-faced woman emerged from the kitchen.

"Yes?"

"Hello," I began, attempting a friendly smile. The woman's glacial demeanour intensified. "I need some help. Can I use your phone? My mobile won't work here –"

"We're not a charitable institution," she interrupted in a nasal whine. "There's a phone outside. Use that."

"I tried that. I've got no change left."

"Buy a drink and I'll give you some change."

"Here's the thing," I said glumly. "When I set off, I didn't bring my wallet. I didn't expect to need money."

"Really?" Her hideous grin revealed a week's work for a dentist. "What planet are you from? On this one we use money to buy goods and services."

The three old blokes found this highly amusing.

"Please," I muttered. "I've had a rough couple of days."

"You a beggar?"

"No, I'm a teacher."

"A teacher?" she squawked. "You're wagging, Sonny. School here closed, years ago."

"I am staying at the Outdoor Ed place –"

Ugly sarcasm became naked hatred in a heartbeat. "Get out!"

"No, please…"

"I said get out. We don't want your snake oil salesman bullshit here."

"I don't understand. I haven't done any harm to you."

"Anyone hooked up with them mongrel thievin' bastards up there is not welcome in this hotel or this town. Get out or I'm callin' the coppers."

"Why do you hate the place so much?"

The woman turned on her heel and marched back through the door from which she emerged. "Gaz!" I heard her strident call. "Gaz. C'mere."

"Them buggers come 'ere," wheezed the first codger at the bar, "said they'd put the place on the map." He sniffed loudly.

A police officer lumbered into the bar, gut straining his shirt.

"You come to fix us up for the camp debts?" he smirked. He paused and added. "Didn't think so."

"Officer," I began, my temple starting to throb. Swelling anger threatened to make me say and do things I would regret later. "My colleagues and I arrived at the Outdoor Ed Centre yesterday. There were no staff present, our phones don't work, we have no way of administering our program, we can't contact school and our only car is out of action."

"Sure, son. How did you get here? Walk?" He roared with laughter.

"Well, I jogged most of the way, actually –"

More riotous laughter cut me off.

"Mate," chortled the woman. She snorted loudly, quivering from the rare entertainment. "You ain't a teacher. You're a bloody comedian."

"But it's true. I –"

"Listen, pal," said the policeman. "Enough of the bullshit. We don't have the time of day here for bastards that do runners and leave people bankrupt. If you have no business in this town, then I suggest you get on your bike and fuck off out of it."

"Is there some way I can get a lift back to camp?"

"If that's really where you're goin', you're wastin' yer time," essayed the fossil on the end of the bar. "No one goes there."

"No one? Isn't there a taxi?"

"Taxi company's shut. No work for 'im."

"My colleague's car needs four new tyres. We could pay you when –"

"Sure," sneered the woman. "That's what them other bludgers said."

"Why won't you believe me?"

The policeman must have sensed a genuine note in my plaintive tone. He pointed to a business card pinned to the board behind the bar. The woman reached for it and thrust it towards me.

"If you know this bloke," he rumbled, "I can't vouch for your safety."

It was a mug shot of Graham Fleming.

"Never seen him before in my life," I heard myself say.

I left the hotel running, sudden adrenalin helping me put distance between me and this surreal den of hatred. I pounded down the main street past the service station and headed for the open road, the jabbing in my side returning. Hitch-hiking back to the city meant breaching Duty of Care and leaving my four colleagues in the lurch. Maddy was one of my colleagues.

Before me in the dirt lay an abandoned mountain bike.

Tuesday, 8.30 p.m.

"Peter!" said Maddy, leaping to her feet. "You're back. You look all in."

My other three colleagues turned to see me trip on an upturned paver and fall on my face, the stone cool on my burning cheeks. Tony lifted me into a chair. Doc passed me a litre of water. My temples throbbed; the world was spinning. Kids gathered. Pain intensified.

"It's Moon," gasped one of the boys.

"Give Mr Moon some space," Victoria demanded.

"Where's he been?"

"What did he do?"

"Why –?"

"Time to go inside," Tony ordered. "Tomorrow is another day."

Muted complaint dissipated. The pounding in my head receded. Maddy wrapped a blanket around me, the best possible medicine. I outlined my day.

"Our esteemed former principal has made some money on this place," said Doc, breaking the hush that followed. "Ron and Naomi must know that."

"But maybe not the part about him not paying his bills," Tony added.

"The last camp went ahead without incident," Victoria noted archly. "No doubt there were camp personnel."

"There was everything but the welcoming red carpet," Tony mused.

"It was there for all to see on Facebook," Doc observed, "for those with time and inclination to log on. It appears the largesse did not extend to us."

"We're on our own," said Victoria.

"In more ways than one, I believe," Tony added grimly.

"I'm paranoid enough to sniff a set-up as well," said Doc.

"Me too," Victoria concurred. "I wouldn't it past that creep Ferrier."

"Depends on how much they actually know," Tony added. "They probably threw money at the other camps to make sure they went well."

"We know about Happy Vale slush funds," Doc commented. "Imagine the irony. They actually spent money on kids, albeit those needing it least."

"That adds up," Victoria grated.

"How will they use it against us?" I was too tired to think.

"Threat of poor performance," Doc pronounced. "Kids complain to parents, who complain to Ferrier. We get carpeted. Our objections are dismissed in paperwork to the department. We go to the union head office, which makes noise, but are ignored. They don't push it as far as actual prosecution, because their case is ultimately flimsy. It is written up very unfavourably. Ferrier adds it to the files they keep on us."

"Files?" Maddy gaped. She studied her phone and frowned in irritation.

"Oh, yes," said Doc. "As we are permanently employed, we are hard to remove, but Ferrier has kept a record of any dissent we have shown."

"What about me?" Maddy interposed.

"Since you dared seek compensation for the 'accident'," said Tony, "they probably opened one on you."

"Naomi has hated you since the start," Victoria scowled.

"You kid me," Maddy whispered.

"She's jealous," Victoria stated. "You have everything she doesn't. Talent. Good looks. Genuine respect from the kids."

"What about me?" I asked.

"You're as fucked as us," Doc observed cheerfully. He turned to Victoria. "And you, dear lady. But our files have been open longer."

"Why does Ron shut his eyes to what goes on?" Maddy demanded.

"It's the path of least resistance for the invertebrate," said Doc.

"How does ignoring the school's obvious problems help him?" Maddy reiterated. "Surely Council won't recommend him for re-appointment."

"The sad fact is," said Doc, "that it's quite likely they will. Ferrier has sat on the School Council extensively and is well known to them. He makes all the right noises and none of the parents ever see what happens at school. The worst parents barge into the Front Office and make scenes about how various teachers are picking on their baby, who is the model of an ideal child. Admin smooths them over and sends them away with platitudes. Graham was brilliant at it. Ferrier and Miss Meredith have learnt well from the master."

"How could they explain away the Fire Drill?" Maddy probed. "It was chaos."

"Simple. The bell went off by mistake and some kids thought they were dismissed. They apologised for the confusion and insisted no damage was done: broken windows fixed, all graffiti removed in record time."

"They tidied up other messes too, with convenient explanations," Tony added. "Did you hear what really happened to Steve Royston?"

"Apart from the broken leg?" Maddy asked. "I helped pull him out of the bottom of the mosh pit when the roll call got out of hand on the oval."

"That was the least of his problems," Doc remarked. "They had him on Duty of Care. He was supposed to be with his Year Elevens when the bell went for the Fire

Drill, but he was still on the phone to the union about his senior self-reliance camp."

"The one when Chad Robertson, Tim Lucas and Robbie Wallis refused to ride their bikes up a hill," Tony added. "They went missing and were found by one of the parents later, blind drunk, in the local pub with fake ID. Steve copped an avalanche of parental complaint. Ferrier held it over his head, on pain of disclosing his failure to maintain appropriate control."

"When he got off the phone to the union," Victoria added, "the riot had started. He got caught in the main group, well away from his class."

"Four of the girls in his class were touched up in the crush," Doc drawled. "They complained to Naomi."

"Naomi added it to the case they had on him," Victoria continued. "It's one of the grievances I have been dealing with. He was stood down indefinitely. He's not allowed to come near us, while this thing drags on. I'm not even supposed to talk about it, but it's so unjust it makes me burn."

Tony got up and had a brief look inside the dorms.

"All quiet," he said on his return.

"We have to occupy the kids until Friday," Maddy declared.

"Any ideas?" Tony asked wearily.

"Spin the planet twice," Doc muttered. "Make it Thursday night."

"Have you eaten anything, Peter?" asked Victoria.

"Not since I tried to ring school," I replied.

"I'll find you something," she said and bustled off to the barbecue.

"Miss?" Annika appeared, the remnants of her almost unrecognisable pink Ugg boots partially covering her feet. "Have you got any more Band-Aids?"

Maddy sighed. "In the red box near the barbecue, Annika. Get them, then go to the dorm. Tomorrow is a busy day."

"What are we doing?" she asked. "Is it anything good?"

"You'll find out tomorrow," said Tony. "Inside."

"Worst camp ever," she complained, retreating.

"Agreed," Doc breathed.

"How did the orienteering go?" I asked.

"It got us to lunch," said Tony. "Then it got messy."

"The injury count was high," Doc added, giving me his full attention. I sensed a new respect for me in his tone. "It seems the cherubs are not accustomed to so much walking. The blisters were only out-numbered by the complaints. Maddy had to deal with the ones who ran off from the exercise, came back here and tried to hide."

"Trying to get them to take the self-reliance aspect seriously was virtually impossible," said Victoria, handing me a warmed lamb chop in bread.

"Just like our fearless leaders," Doc observed.

"How can kids learn responsibility," Maddy demanded, visibly perturbed by the insights of the day, "when they feel they can do as they like? How can true freedom exist without responsibility?"

"It can in The Happy Vale High Book of Rights," Doc smiled wryly, "but No Responsibilities."

"That's so cynical," Maddy murmured. "But –"

"It's not wrong either," Victoria chimed in.

"It's the fault of the teacher," Doc dead-panned, as he winced, popped one of his pills and drank from his glass of water. "I am sure we'll hear about it next week, when aggrieved parents point out our failings to Executive."

"Like they did after Pete's issue last year with Samara," said Tony.

"Samara Glascott?" Maddy interjected. "One of the Specials?"

"That one is most assuredly in the file of Mr Moon," Doc intoned.

"I ended up on the floor covered by a quarter of Year Nine," I clarified, "after I interrupted 'Stacks on the Mill' in one of Elspeth's classes."

"Where was Elspeth?" Maddy queried, sounding faint. She switched her phone off with an aggravated stab of her thumb.

"In the Lotus Position in our office," I said. "You were at a conference."

"What happened?"

"They jumped on me when I tried to get kids off Samara. Rambo turned up with Mary and it took the rest of the lesson to restore sanity."

"I happened to be in the front office first thing next day," said Doc, "when the parents came roaring in.

Naomi took them into her office. I lingered and managed to overhear most of it. Apparently young Mr Moon here was aggressive toward their children. They wanted to press criminal charges."

"What?" Maddy gasped. "That's in the diary too?"

"Naturally," Doc stated gravely. "They covered for Elspeth. She had been called to take an important phone call. Young Mr Moon had heard a disturbance and misread a Drama game. Mr Ferrier assured the parents that Mr Moon had undertaken professional development over a judgement error and had been offered counselling."

"There won't be any cover for us," Tony warned. "Whatever crap the more melodramatic parents spout to Ron and Naomi, we will have to wear it. The longer Travis and Damien are on the loose, the worse it is for us."

"In my spare moments this morning," Doc said, "I added to our journal. Before I retire tonight, I will sum up your unfortunate experiences today."

"Too bad you didn't get the cop's number," Victoria lamented.

"You described him well enough earlier," Doc added. "I'll be sure to quote his words for the edification of our esteemed leaders."

Parked corpse-like in the chair, trying not to intensify the agony in my backside from the fifty kilometre ride back to camp, I grunted assent.

"Apple juice?" Doc offered at large.

"Not for me," said Maddy, standing, her swollen ankle still troubling her. "I'm going to bed."

"Me too," said Victoria. "Good night."

"I'll have a quick look around the area," said Tony.

He got up and switched on his torch. We sat in silence as his footsteps receded. Doc poured me a generous shot of scotch and then one for himself. Tony returned, accepted another shot and settled into his chair.

"The boys are pretty quiet," Tony observed eventually.

"Is that a good thing?" Doc queried. "Instinct says no."

"We need to keep watch into the night, Doc," Tony suggested. "Pete. You're excused. Have a shower and get to bed."

Cascading hot water caressed me in the shower, then cut out. Light snapped off. The shock of cold water hit. The way forward fell dark and dangerous, just like my first year at Happy Vale. Too tired to question it further, I hurriedly dried myself, felt my way to my bunk, crawled into my sleeping bag and expired.

Wednesday, 3.00 a.m.

Slow motion threats loomed. Disembodied sound edged inward. Weightlessness receded before gravity and reality. Swelling suffering in every bodily cell awakened me. A sliver of moonlight streaked the floor.

The undercurrent of murmuring from next door drifted past the mass of Tony in his sleeping bag. The boys were awake; at least, some of them were. Muffled sniggering confirmed my suspicions.

"Gimme the bong." That was Travis.

Adrenalin flowed as I spilled from bunk to floor. The small sounds from next door ceased. My legs and buttocks were cauldrons of lactic acid and my head encased a fog of such intense pain that my eyes, wrung dry from the loss of bodily fluid, filled anew with salty tears. The contents of my stomach were suddenly in my mouth, my knees gave way and I heaved great gouts of vomit onto the floor. Cold sweat returned to blur what vision remained. Scuttling footfalls vanished into the night.

"Pete?" I heard Tony, his voice heavy with sleep. "Pete?"

My eyes were dazzled by Tony's torch beam in my face.

"Travis was here," I croaked. "I heard him."

I struggled to my feet and tried the light switch.

"Power's off," Tony whispered.

The sour stench of vomit filled my nostrils. Tony pulled his tracksuit on, stepped outside and returned with a bucket and rags. I took them and roughly wiped the worst of it from the floor.

"I can't see Doc," Tony whispered.

My eyes had adjusted enough to the dimness to see that Doc's bunk was empty. My head swam with the misery of my pain and my body screamed in silent protest at the torture it had undergone. Outside, the moon was clear and deep silence had descended again.

"What should we do?" I whispered, as Tony joined me.

"We need to check if all the boys are there," he murmured, "without disturbing the sleeping ones. Then we need to find Doc."

Tony crept back through the entrance to the main dorm. He played his torch along the upper reaches of the walls, gradually working past each of the double bunks. There were three empty beds.

"Trent, Blake and Tristan," I whispered.

"You're right," said Tony, killing the light. We withdrew to our ante-room.

Every sound of pulling on my tracksuit and Nikes seemed amplified. The outrage in my stomach triggered acid reflux in my mouth. My blistered feet protested. We paused and listened. The dorm seemed quiet again. We crept into the moonlight.

"Man, I'm so hungry," said a voice softly from the barbecue area.

"There ain't no fuckin' food here, man," I heard another voice say. There was a brief muffled parley.

"There must be," whispered the first voice.

"Someone's coming," said another.

"Stay where you are," I demanded.

Footsteps thudded on the pavers and on through the scrub around the edge of the camp to continue crashing through the bush. New adrenalin momentarily over-rode my pain. Distant sounds of feet disturbing the forest floor said the boys were well clear of camp.

Failure to grab my torch made me pause to take in my surroundings. The moon had retreated behind cloud and the trees closed me in. I moved on and immediately slipped, falling awkwardly, jarring my knee and scratching my forehead.

"Fuck!" A voice cried somewhere ahead.

My blistered feet protested with each step through intimidating blackness and dread of each low branch or hole. The moon peered from behind a cloud. Eyes adjusted to the dark, I turned in the direction of the distant profanities and continued.

Damien, Travis, Trent, Blake and Tristan were less than a kilometre away. The stowaways must have found shelter, but had no food, hence the raid on camp. The path wound deeper into the bush. Adrenalin faded; fatigue and pain returned. My head hit something hard.

Occasional shouts pierced the night. Looking up at the moon, I missed my footing, slipped, and toppled down a slope to land heavily some metres below the path. Pain overwhelmed me.

Everything faded to grey.

Wednesday, 6.15 a.m.

"It's Moon."

"Is he dead?"

"If he isn't, we could kill him. No one would know."

My blood seemed to freeze. The aching stabbed internally. Silhouettes loomed above in the half light. Clods of earth fell nearby. A heavier load of dirt and detritus slid down the slope.

"Trav," I heard a voice whisper. "You burying him?"

"Shut up and help me."

"Push. Push."

"What are you doing, Trav?"

"Push."

Another small avalanche of dirt fell on top of me, then another and another still. The dirt filled my mouth and hands were trapped under me by its weight. More came down and threatened to engulf me. A stone bounced off my nose and I tasted fresh blood.

"Trav," repeated the voice. "You can't kill him. People will find out."

"No they won't." That was Blake.

"He got me suspended," Travis continued, "when I didn't do nothin'."

"Trav, are you fuckin' crazy? It's murder."

"No-one will know. He's a fuckin' arsehole. I hate him."

"Trav," Blake said. "Those rocks'll cover 'im."

"You can't kill him." That was Tristan.

"I'm not killin' him. I'm makin' him have an accident. Stiff shit."

"The cops'll come and look. They'll find his body."

"There's no fingerprints. It'll look like an accident."

"What about Friday? When the bus comes?"

"Shut up, ya dick…"

He said something else, inaudible due to more sliding dirt. A stone bounced off my head. My world was a fog of agony. Crushing weight bore down on my chest, dirt in my eyes, mouth and nose. Twisting my body eased pressure on my lungs and ribcage, but blood filled my nose. Panic threatened to overwhelm me. I managed a sobbing breath and struggled to spit out the choking blood and dirt. Suddenly lack of consultation in staff meetings didn't seem so bad.

The voices were gone. A new fire began burning within. Travis Armour was trying to kill me. Rage lent me strength. Gradually I squirmed to free my arms, numb from being trapped under my body.

A ten-second converted text message for Mrs Armour: "Hello? Mrs Armour? Peter Moon. Your son has just tried to bury me alive. I'm afraid this contravenes the tenets of Affirmative Education…"

No sound broke the dawn stillness. My body, pushed beyond all normal limits, screamed in every fibre for release. The crushing weight eased. Finally clear of my premature grave, jarred knee throbbing, limbs burning, stomach churning, limping back to camp, only rage kept me moving as I contemplated the boy who thought he could get away with murder.

Maddy had forgiven him for throwing the brick that smashed the window and scarred her face with its vicious shards.

The morning was clear, air crisp, birds chirped; Mother Nature mocked me. The path appeared trodden before. It took another twenty minutes of tracking back and forth before the right path to camp revealed itself. I almost missed seeing Doc, half-buried in the undergrowth.

Wednesday, 9.00 a.m.

Doc was dead.

Dead. Ceased to be, as Doc loved to say, quoting Monty Python. Bereft of life, but definitely not resting in peace. In the rictus of expiry, his face was frozen in the act of speech, agony evident.

What were his last words? Were the last syllables he uttered choked by cardiac seizure? Did he waste the final spark of his eloquence on Travis?

On my knees, I choked out sobs over the shell of the sage who had jollied me through the half-decade of disillusionment that was my professional career to date. No more pearls before swine. Doc's light was out.

Where was justice? What happened to fair play? How was it that this erudite, wise, cultured soul should suffer such an unseemly demise? Think of the morons who litter Nine News each evening: murderers, wife beaters, drug dealers, hit-and-run drivers, breakers-and-enterers… the unprincipled lawless who use violence to take from the innocent. Here I was, in the wild, chasing apprentice criminals who would evolve into the kind of Happy Vale alumni that Doc listed during his penultimate night on earth. This was the kind of apprentice criminal whom Maddy found it possible to forgive. How?

Fuck.

"FUUUUUUUCK!"

I wept in desolation. My brain throbbed, my body jerked in spasms of misery.

Filthy, blood-stained, I slipped back into camp. Washing in cold water I bit back involuntary gasps. Tony, Maddy and Victoria found me in the dorm.

"What is it?" Victoria asked. I convulsed in grief again.

"What?" demanded Maddy.

"Doc," Tony whispered. I shuddered deeply and nodded.

Maddy and Victoria gripped each other's hands in horror. All four of us clung together. No one spoke.

"Miss Ambrose?" Annika's voice drifted inside. "Where are you? I need more Band-Aids. Miss Ambrose!"

Maddy took a deep breath, ran a tissue over her eyes, blew her nose and called out: "Just a moment, Annika. I think I know where there are a few."

All business, Maddy hobbled into the other room. Victoria stared at me, trying to say something and failing.

"Pete," whispered Tony. "We have to –"

"I know."

"Maddy and I will hold the fort," Victoria offered. "Go."

Tony and I slipped away from camp and covered Doc in a disused tarpaulin, concealing his resting place with leaves and assorted bush deadfall.

"Poor old bastard," Tony sobbed.

"It was Travis," I grated. "He did this –"

"You don't know that –"

"It was fucking Travis!"

"We have to pull ourselves together," Tony insisted, wiping his eyes with his handkerchief and blowing his nose noisily. He heaved a massive sigh. "We can't hide this for long. We'll say he went for help."

"Is that the best we've got?"

"It's all I've got," Tony admitted.

Victoria jemmied the office door open with the tyre lever from her car. We were unsurprised to find the office phone dead. In the shed behind the office the generator had died as well and there was nothing to fuel it. The fridge in the office contained nothing other than an empty ice cube tray.

There were no candles in the cupboards, nor were there reserve gas cylinders for the barbecue. There was only one long-life milk in the otherwise empty cupboard. However, there was a piano in the recreation room. Maddy ruled that it was in tune.

Reality bit.

Phones were dead. TV and internet were non-existent. We had limited food, no power, no hot water and no passive entertainment.

"This has become a bush music camp," Maddy announced to the silent throng. "You guys are my new choir."

Excited chatter broke out. It wasn't exactly a 1930s-style Great Depression stoic acceptance of hardship, but petulance was melting before unexpected resilience.

"I'll be buggered," whispered Tony.

Suddenly I felt worthless. My endeavours had amounted to nothing. My trip to town had been an exhausting failure. My nocturnal blundering had facilitated the escape of the renegades, which had led to Doc's death. Blackness clouded my mind, then the red furnace of rage. I stepped outside.

Wednesday, 11.30 a.m.

"No jury would convict me."

"Pete," shouted Tony, gasping for breath as he laboured to keep up. "Get a grip. Just hold on."

"That little shit has Doc's blood on his hands," I snapped. "Time for a little Old Testament justice, I reckon."

"Listen to yourself," Tony gasped. "You won't get away with it. You won't be able to live with yourself."

"They practically get away with murder every day at school," I shouted. "Now they're doing it for real."

"We don't know that," Tony tried to reason. "Pete, stop, or you'll give me heart failure too."

"Did I tell you that Travis tried to kill me?"

My blistered feet screamed silently, while Tony's determined shuffle to stay in touch gradually receded behind. He stopped talking, recognising the futility of logic. Besides, he needed all his breath to keep me in sight. I plunged on, oblivious to anything other than the red mist in my brain.

"Pete," Tony gasped. "Hold it."

"What new opportunities for personal growth and professional learning have you scoped this year?" I shouted back at him, quoting Sam's opening words at the most recent staff meeting. I stopped, doubled over and dry-retched. Tony caught up.

"Give it a rest," Tony panted.

"Rage and depression!" I shouted, after my dry heaving subsided. "They are the opportunities that Affirmative Ed has scoped for me."

Nothing less than trapping Travis Armour and putting the fear of God into his heathen soul would be adequate. Consequences were for others: if Travis and his mates were not subject to the law then neither was I.

My sore knee throbbed. The world began to lurch at unnatural angles. Sourness welled inside my gut, my stomach in revolt. I dry-retched the last bile from my empty insides.

"Pete," Tony whispered in my ear. "Come back to camp."

For the second time in half a day Tony hauled my exhausted body upright. Red rage receded. Blackness gave way to grey fatigue. We turned back and pressed on in silence.

After about ten minutes, broken branches on a gum sapling at shoulder height revealed a break in the bush to our left, an accident in the otherwise pristine vegetation. It led to an uphill path well-worn into the gum-studded hillside. The path broadened into a track of sorts, which wound away in a different direction. Four wheel drives must have come this way.

"There must be some kind of ranger's hut or cottage nearby," I whispered to Tony. "My bet is that Travis and company have found it."

"Let me do the talking if we find them," he whispered back.

One part of me acknowledged the sense of it. Another part wanted no more to do with sense. Fatigue ground me down again.

We continued in silence, surprise our only advantage. The hush of the bush was total, until the discreet chirp of a rosella sounded from above. Several birds took off. Small stones bounced off the massive gum tree trunk above and landed near me.

"It's them," I whispered.

"Let me do the talking," Tony repeated, mouthing the words.

We climbed the slope to the tree and began working our way around its broad base, pushing through the lower level scrub and tall grass in time for me to catch a glimpse of colour through the foliage. The runaways led us uphill for several minutes. Behind me, Tony's breath came in ragged gasps.

The sun filtered through the canopy above and I saw that we were approaching a clearing. We stopped before revealing ourselves. Tony was bent double, sucking in great drafts of air. I listened hard. Nothing.

"Let's keep going," I whispered.

The steady climb became less taxing. We appeared to be reaching the summit of a hill. The track was narrow and wound to the left. We kept to the left against the stand of trees and initially failed to notice the ranger's hut in the forest.

"Where are they?" I whispered to myself.

"Don't do anything," Tony urged.

I was already running forward.

Wednesday, 3.30 p.m.

The world began again as a smeared blur of colour. Pain pushed back my first attempt at rising. A more determined attempt to become upright attracted Tony's attention. Three or four versions of him swam in the doorway. The rough bandage on my head failed to relieve throbbing that dwarfed my most preposterous hangover.

Tony spoke as if from far away: "Are you OK?"

Opening my mouth to speak intensified the agony.

Loosely applied, the bandage slid from my forehead. My fingers came away stained by my own drying blood. My feet fell to the floor, which was littered with open tins and dry food packets, discarded food scraps, ants, dead matches, ash, cigarette butts, long-consumed emergency rations.

"What happened?" I croaked. "I remember getting to the door of the cabin, pulling it open, then …"

"You were ambushed," said Tony wryly. He picked up a heavy iron bucket. "This was balanced above the door."

The bucket was stained with my blood. The stones and dirt that weighted it were spread across the floor where they landed, after the trap had been sprung. An old dish served as an ashtray of sorts. Black filth from the tell-tale, abandoned marijuana water pipe on the table smeared its surface, along with some of the ash from the marijuana that had been smoked. The hut stank of it. Doc's now-empty two-litre container of 'apple juice' had been discarded on the floor.

Other than evidence of looting and littering, there was no other sign of the runaways. No possessions other than the bong remained. Not finding Travis and his friends in the ranger hut infuriated me but lent me strength as well. The same could not be said for Tony, but he wasn't letting me go now.

"We should get back," Tony insisted.

"How long was I out for?"

"Quite a while."

"Any sign of the boys?"

"Nope. I looked around the area, but they are well clear."

"When we get back, I'm going to put this in the book. I saw where Doc put it next to his bunk. When we get back to school –"

"OK," Tony interrupted. "OK. Hold on. Yes, I agree it's a sorry tale that must be told, but we need to make sure it's accurate and without emotion. Don't forget, we don't know for sure how Doc died. There will need to be an autopsy. We can't make assumptions. We need our facts to be straight."

As usual, Tony was making sense. The sudden reminder of Doc brought grief and rage to the boil again.

"Pete," Tony implored. "Let's go."

Wednesday, 6.15 p.m.

Exhaustion slowed us both. Fading light played havoc with our sense of direction and more than once we took a wrong turn. Maddy stood in the firelight, Victoria at the barbecue. Cooking aromas reminded me that I was desperately hungry.

Tristan stood before Maddy, his back to us. Near him by the fire was Trent, sporting a serious shiner. An angry noise erupted from my throat. Heads turned.

"Mr Moon?" Karen gasped. "Are you OK?"

The shocked gaze of all present fell upon my blood and dirt-caked appearance. A babble of voices erupted.

"Pete," Tony whispered. "Get inside and clean up. You're a mess."

Icy cold shower water had me swiftly cleansed and outside again. Tristan was talking while the group listened. When he saw me he stopped.

"Tristan," Maddy said. "Go on."

"Trav said he'd cut my eyes out if I dobbed," Tristan continued, his voice shaking. "He pulled out the big knife he used to slash Miss Green's car tyres. He keeps it in his belt. Him 'n' Blake 'n' Damien used it to become blood brothers. But I didn't want him cuttin' my arm with it –"

"Me neither," Trent added. He glanced my way, looking ready to bolt. Tony's stilling hand was by my side.

"It's all right, now, Tristan," Tony soothed. "You have made a wise decision to come back to camp. You, too, Trent."

"I don't want Trav comin' near me," Tristan averred.

"Stay close to camp now," said Victoria. "Don't go anywhere alone."

"I'm scared," said Karen. "What if they come at night?"

A swelling chorus of voices underscored the fear that Karen had spoken aloud. Maddy held her hands up for silence. The voices trailed away.

"We'll stick together," she said simply. "Right now we need to tidy up the barbecue area."

"I'll wash," said Sarah. She rose, bustled to the improvised outdoor sink, a big plastic tub, and took it to the rainwater tank.

"I'll help," said Annika loudly. She followed, her feet wrapped in multiple layers of socks, pink Ugg boots nowhere to be seen.

"After we clean up," said Maddy, "let's all go to the piano. "We can run through the songs we learnt today until we lose the light."

There was general movement towards helping with the clean-up and also to the dorms. Tony and I helped ourselves to the remnants of the cooling barbecue meat and the last of the salad and bread rolls. Trent and Tristan joined us, still hungry after the privations of outlaw-dom.

"What are they doing now, Tristan?" Victoria asked.

"I dunno," the boy answered, as he devoured the last of a barbecued chicken breast. "They said they wanted to piss off North, but they needed food."

"Do you think they'll come back here tonight?"

"Maybe," said Trent, shoving a barbecued sausage into his mouth and speaking through it. "All the food in the hut is gone."

"Tristan," Maddy probed, "is there anything else you can tell us about Travis, Blake and Damien?"

"Trav's gone psycho," replied Tristan. "And Blake. Damo's gone quiet. He's Trav's best bud, but Blake's started pushing him to one side..."

"Go on," said Tony.

"I dunno –"

"He's right," Trent said, glowering. "Blake bashed me for givin' Mr Moon the shanghais. His older brother wanted them back. He smashed me in the face."

"Do you think Damien might come back?" Tony asked quietly.

"Nah," said Trent. "He hasn't had his tablets all week. He's more psycho than Trav. Besides, they've still got plenty of weed stashed. He swapped most of his tablets for his share, so he won't be leavin' yet."

"Mr Amadio?" Karen called from her washing up. "Where's Doc Cooper?"

"He went for help," said Tony, not daring to glance in my direction.

"When did he do that?" she asked.

Several other kids eyed Tony. I glanced at Trent and Tristan. Neither seemed to react to the mention of Doc.

"Earlier today," Tony replied.

"I didn't see him," said Sarah.

"No," Tony said.

"Which way did he go?" Annika asked.

"An … other way," I said, perhaps a little too quickly. "From … where I went, I mean. There's another town. He went … that way."

"Oh," said Annika.

The girls finished cleaning up and went inside. Travis and Trent followed, apparently innocent of any involvement in Doc's death. Tony's eyes followed them. He shrugged in my direction and stood to go inside as well.

I trudged to my bunk, spent. Song from next door calmed me, but sleep took time to come.

Thursday, 10.00 a.m.

My one minute dousing in an ever-decreasing gravity stream of chilly underground water refreshed me a little, but Doc's death weighed intolerably. Empty reassurances that Doc might return with help were acid in my mouth.

We had to ration the small amount of remaining food supplies on the penultimate day. It looked like we would all miss breakfast on the final morning. The original plan was for Victoria to drive to town halfway through the week to top up supplies. That seemed like a hundred years ago.

"That's the end of the cordial," said Sarah, dropping the last empty two litre container into the bin. Karen emerged from the office with empty bottles and used paper plates and headed for the bin as well.

"And tea," Victoria lamented. She tossed a reused teabag onto one of the paper plates as Karen passed.

"And the coffee," Tony added glumly, rinsing his cup in the cold water basin. The rainwater tanks are very low as well."

"Fill your water bottles," said Maddy. "We'll have to share what's left."

In orderly silence, the kids complied. Tony tapped the large tank's exterior and shook his head. The smaller one was already drained dry.

"Make your water last until the afternoon," Tony announced. "We may only have one refill left each."

Teens accustomed to high caffeine energy drinks, iced coffee and Coke quietly assented. Trent and Tristan acted as monitors, making sure there was no spillage. When everyone had taken water, the tank appeared to be all but empty.

"What now?" Sarah asked, breaking the silence.

"Choir practice," said Maddy.

"Singing might make us thirsty, Miss," Annika suggested.

"Not if you breathe properly," said Maddy. "Come on."

Obediently, the majority stood and followed Maddy and Victoria into the room with the piano. A group of a dozen boys had discovered chess sets in the past day. They settled around the campfire area and recommenced the camp chess championships. Four others went inside to get the camp's two small axes and wheelbarrow, set to accompany Tony gathering wood for our final evening campfire.

The boys wheeled the barrow into the clearing, but Tony lingered, strained, exhausted, regarding me as I pulled on my Nikes.

"I'm not coming with you," he mouthed. "Don't do anything stupid."

"I've created new levels of stupid, Tony," I muttered. "I doubt I can top myself this time."

"If you find them," Tony muttered, "just keep it low-key. Point out we're only here for another day. They need to be here when the bus comes for us. There's no point in harbouring anger. You'll only make it worse for yourself."

"You're right, of course," I assented.

"Think about it," said Tony. "When they come back, they won't want to advertise that they ran off. They'll pressure their friends to say nothing. The other kids will get the word to keep it quiet."

"No one else knows," I added, thinking it though.

"Tell them to come back and all will be forgiven."

"No consequences for their behaviour, as usual –"

"We're stuck with it."

Hot anger welled and I paced furiously.

"Can you actually contemplate forgiving them?"

"Pete, calm down. What is the point of going off at them? It's not going to change anything. It's not going to –"

"– bring Doc back!" I whispered fiercely. "I'm over this. We have to tell Ferrier and Naomi what happened."

"We don't know what happened. We can only give them the facts. Anyway, what are Ferrier and Naomi going to do?" Tony arched an eyebrow.

"Nothing, of course." I sighed in recognition of the inevitable.

"This is a situation out of the ordinary. Last night after you went to bed Victoria and I talked it over. We are going to get stuck into Naomi and Ferrier over sending us off on this disaster waiting to happen. We will accuse them of allowing you to travel alone with fifty kids, in the full knowledge that there was no replacement for Steve Royston. We'll condemn them for knowing that the place was unstaffed. And we'll consult lawyers over Doc's death, to nail them over making him do this camp against his doctor's orders."

"But –"

"We say nothing about the runaways. We drop them off near their homes, before we get back to school."

"Huh," my breath exhaled in bitterness.

"Think about it," Tony insisted. "We keep it quiet they were here. They keep quiet about their antics. No one suffers."

"I suppose so," I mumbled darkly. Keeping quiet fell well short of forgiveness.

"Don't take more than three hours," he urged.

"I'll be back by early afternoon," I promised

Thursday, 12.00 p.m.

The hut was abandoned, only mess remaining. The rainwater tank outside was low, but had enough to fill my bottle. Could the boys have decided to return to camp? Had any of the rosellas been unlucky enough to be hit by a stone for its stringy flesh?

Dense scrub lined the track back to camp. A narrow path through the trees continued uphill on the other side of the hut. I climbed until sunlight in the forest crown showed an opening, where I almost stepped into space.

Thick bush extended on all sides below the cliff-top. Ahead of me stretched a glorious vista, a primeval paradise untouched now as it was before our European ancestors began populating the continent. At least until Happy Vale entered the forest.

Below was a deep valley. Across it arose more inaccessible highlands towering almost vertically from the valley floor, skyscrapers of rock, earth and timber. The wilderness stretched North, a deep green haze of crags and valleys. A play of light below caught my eye: running water.

Any path must surely lead to Travis, Blake and Damien. An open hillside behind a layer of dense scrub revealed itself, when a wallaby hopped from the undergrowth. I began slipping and sliding down. The scent of fresh water floated on the breeze. I tied a piece of my handkerchief to a branch to mark the place.

To the north a low bubbling sound led to the bank of a steadily flowing creek, at least ten metres wide and a metre or more deep in its middle. Across it lay a towering rock wall. There might be caves, or at least natural shelters underneath innumerable tonnes of rock. The watercourse bent away to the left downstream.

The sun was halfway across the western sky as I came upon a small beach beside a bend in the creek near a rocky overhang. It could be a shelter in adverse weather. Other potential shelters became visible.

At school it was home time. If I had toed the line and not associated with the dissidents, I might have been already on my way to the car-park, en route to the pub. I would endure nothing more testing than an ear-bashing from Gaz about how he was raking in the dollars, before a good night's sleep in my comfortable bed, with just a few lessons between me and glorious weekend. As always, though, the bells of Monday morning would toll again for me and my colleagues and the fading dream of Making a Difference.

Hours late back to camp, no contact made, afternoon wearing on, yet duty still whispered. Or was it bloody-mindedness? Tony seemed to be advocating a discreet kind of clemency. A little over a day ago, Travis Armour was trying to bury me alive. My body ached in unimaginable ways. Numb, I shed yet more tears for Doc.

My anger had burnt out, or so I thought. Travis Armour had tried to kill me. What new opportunities for personal growth and professional learning had I scoped lately? It occurred to me that I might be taking a crash course in vigilante rage and murder. Who would know? I could stalk. Bide my time. Creep close. Strike.

"I couldn't find them, Tony. I tried..."

We would have to report them missing. The cops would comb the area. I would have to make it look like an accident and hide them well. I'd shut up. Meanwhile, we'd report Doc's death. Tony and Victoria would lay it on thick about how the actions of Travis and friends caused Doc to...

Then I saw the footprints.

Thursday, 5.30 p.m.

The wind had picked up from the North. Above to the West, streamers of cloud began massing. The russet glow of sunset smeared the western sky. Smoke floated downwind. Something cooking made my stomach gurgle.

Ahead were two fishing lines, wedged into rocks by the running water. Voices were audible. I edged closer, staying behind the screen of bush. Through the leaves was the spectacle of Travis and Blake gorging themselves on freshly caught fish. My stomach gurgled. Sudden rage gripped me again. At camp we had no food and the stowaways had surplus.

A few words were audible amid the slurping and belching.

"Fuck, this is good."

"Fuck, yeah."

I studied them, David Attenborough-style.

The feral rat-dog inhabits shadowy outcrops, where it gorges itself on the potent weed its over-heated cranial cavity craves...

More fish hissed and bubbled in a cast iron fry pan that sat over a substantial cooking fire. The filthy bong sat next to it, smoke still floating within the plastic tube that led to its mouthpiece.

My stomach gurgled again, loudly.

Sprung.

Both boys leapt to their feet.

"Dude!" shouted Blake.

"What the fuck?" Travis blurted through a mouth full of fish.

I walked towards them, mind racing, heart pounding. Fresh anger at Travis blurred in my mind with Tony's counsel. Travis picked up a large brown-stained knife that might have done Crocodile Dundee proud. He spat out a fishbone and waved the knife in my direction.

"You can fuck off, arsehole," he snarled. "This is our camp. No fuckin' teachers. Get the fuck out of our camp."

"I see you're into Outdoor Ed."

Rage stilled, clemency forgotten, mesmerised by the blade, that was my best.

"I said to fuck off, arsehole," Travis shouted.

Blake sniggered and deliberately packed a fresh cone in the bong, lighting it with a twig from the fire and drawing the smoke deeply into his lungs. The bubbling water sounded clearly over the steady Northerly that buffeted the flames of the cooking fire. He exhaled a stream of marijuana smoke in my direction.

"Travis. Blake. It's Thursday. The buses are coming for us tomorrow."

"Fuck off," Travis brayed. "Arsehole."

"We're not fuckin' goin'," Blake announced.

"What about your families?"

"Fuck 'em."

Blake began packing another cone. The wind gusted more strongly. A shower of sparks from the fire blew away from the surrounding stones.

"We'll have to raise the alarm," I said. "If we leave camp without you, we'll have to report you missing."

"We don't fuckin' care," Travis announced. "Arsehole."

The boys exchanged mirror-image sneers. Blake passed Travis the bong and lit it for him. Travis drew deeply on the burning coal of the drug and exhaled forcefully towards me. Both sets of eyes were red-rimmed and glassy. Blake belched loudly; they lapsed into loud, mocking laughter.

"Where's Damien?" I asked.

Both faces clouded.

"Dunno," Blake mumbled through pursed lips.

"Don't fuckin' care," added Travis. "Arsehole."

"He's a fuckin' pussy," Blake snarled. "We don't like fuckin' pussies."

"He fucked off," Travis spoke in a sing-song tone, while Blake began packing another cone. "Arsehole."

"Hey, Trav," sniggered Blake. "Remember. He's a fuckin' teacher."

"Oh," Travis laughed, an ugly bark. "Right. *Mr* Arsehole."

"Mr Fucking Arsehole."

Travis cackled some more, inhaled the cone and exhaled gustily.

"Boys," I pleaded. "Half the police force will be looking for you."

"Fuck the cops," Travis bellowed.

"Please come back to camp. Nothing will happen to you –"

"Yeah, right," Travis shouted, "Mr Fucking Arsehole. Sure. If I come back, you'll dob me in. I'll be in Juvie next week. Fuck off. Tell 'em you couldn't find us."

"I promise you," I essayed bleakly. "Nothing will happen."

Yes, nothing will happen, as usual at school. I seemed outside my own body, marvelling in some abstract way at the blandness of my words.

"Bullshit!" shouted Blake. "He's fuckin' lyin', like all fuckin' teachers."

Blake picked up a large piece of burning wood and advanced on me with it. Travis came forward as well, slashing the air with his knife, cackling. I was forced back. They kept coming, hunting me.

"Please," I entreated, a corner of my mind aware I was now seeking, not offering clemency.

Blake swung the burning end of the wood at me and made contact with the torn edge of my T-shirt, which caught the flame and held. The fire burnt my torso and I yelped with pain. Travis slashed wildly with his knife. I dodged and felt the fire on my T-shirt again. Sparks flew and I slipped.

"Get him!" Travis snarled.

Blake lunged at me with the burning brand and the flame seared my forearm. I gasped in pain and scrambled away. He jabbed at me again and made contact with my T-shirt. Travis slashed at me with his knife, cutting me on the other forearm. Suddenly my T-shirt was on fire. Travis cut me again on my chest. I snapped, swinging my foot up and kicking him full in the stomach.

"Fucking shit!" He doubled over, coughing and dropped the knife.

Blake grabbed it and came at me with knife and burning brand, which made contact with my chest and right arm. My T-shirt was on fire and the flames scorched me. I cried out in agony, tore the T-shirt off and jumped into the cold stream. The strong, hot wind gusted my T-shirt away.

Travis was vomiting his gorged fish into the sand. He picked himself up and rushed to the creek's edge. I ducked under the water to gain relief from the hideous pain of my burns.

"I'll kill you, Arsehole." He clutched at his stomach and yelped in pain. "I'll fucking get you for this, you fucking Arsehole. I'll fucking kill you."

Where was my iPhone with its video camera when I needed it?

Blake danced a jig of victory.

"Fuck off, Arsehole."

"*Mr* Arsehole."

"Mr *Fucking* Arsehole."

I waded upstream, burnt, bleeding from the cuts, away from the pair, plunging through water, wanting distance between us now, keeping my burns in the water as much as possible. I had failed again. There had been no acceptance by Travis and Blake that the game was up, no cessation of hostility, truce and the closure it offered, no forgiveness. I had found them, but they refused to return. In Ferrier's book, that was failure in my Duty of Care.

Eventually I found the point at which I had discovered the creek. The searing pain from my burns intensified seconds after I crawled out of the water. Blood still seeped from the cuts on my still-wet chest and arms. Light was fading, likewise hope.

Uphill, where my handkerchief marked the way out, darkness had fallen. I climbed the hill to the cliff-top. There was smoke on the North wind.

Down in the valley to the North-West a fire was blazing in the bush.

Thursday, 9.30 p.m.

Shirtless, shivering, wounded, burnt, exhausted, famished, I blundered through the darkness and lost my way a number of times. In camp all was quiet. Tony sat alone by the remains of the campfire.

"Bloody Hell," he exploded, before pulling his voice back to an undertone. "We'd just about given you for lost."

"What's happening?" I muttered, slumping into a vacant outdoor chair.

"Everyone's asleep," said Tony, gaping. "What happened to you?"

"Least of our problems," I sighed.

"Well?"

"I found them."

"And –?"

Tony listened, open-mouthed. Tuesday *had* been the worst day of my life. Wednesday and Thursday had relegated Tuesday back to the Bronze medal position. I saved mention of the potential bushfire until last. Tony slapped his hand over his face.

"How far off is it?"

"It's in the far valley," I said. "Hopefully it won't spread."

"We can't evacuate the camp," Tony agonised. "Not in total darkness."

"We can see what's happening at first light," I suggested. "The wind isn't strong right now."

"Yeah, but from what you said, it's blowing this way."

We sat in silence for a moment. My stomach rumbled loudly.

"Any food left?"

"Sorry."

Friday, 6.15 a.m.

Despite my exhaustion, sleep proved elusive. The cuts and burns would have done that by themselves, but my injuries did not cut and burn as much as my abject failure to bring Travis and Blake back, let alone find occasion to forgive.

I couldn't forgive myself.

Tony was up before me, regardless. At first light we were scanning the horizon to the North. Victoria and Maddy joined us. I pushed self-recriminations to one side and summed up the imminent threat.

By breakfast time, the kids all sat about the campfire area, despite the knowledge that they would be going hungry. The topic of Doc appeared taboo. Refraining from any mention of his name had spread to the kids. The whispering stopped whenever any adult came into earshot.

The morning air lacked freshness. The northerly, which had sprung up again at first light, blew harder, sky to the north smudged brown. Unease informed every movement, every anxious glance. Tony joined me in the clearing.

"We've got to go," I whispered. "That fire is coming this way."

"We have to make it orderly," he murmured. "Kids have been good these past two days, but the thought of a bushfire –"

"Agreed," said Victoria. "Maddy and I will round up the girls."

"What about –?" My eyes indicated North.

"If the fire doesn't drive them this way," said Tony, "they'll be cooked."

"We've got ninety-seven other kids to worry about," said Victoria.

We made our way to the camp area. The kids regarded us silently.

"I'm thirsty," Annika complained.

"Have a sip of my bottle," said Trent, offering it.

"Thanks," she said and took a small mouthful.

"Listen up," Tony instructed. "The northerly is blowing a fire this way."

Gasps and cries of dismay interrupted.

"Shut up!" Trent shouted. "Listen to Mr Amadio."

"We have no choice," Tony continued. "We need to leave now."

Fingers pointed North. A babble of voices repeated my question.

"We leave in one minute," Tony announced. "Get your things. Leave anything you can't carry. We walk down that path. Orderly. Together. Questions?"

There were none. Tony went into the male dorm to check if anyone had missed the announcement. Smoke and heat haze were visible in the sky to the North. Maddy and Victoria hurried the last of the girls from the female dorm. Tony re-appeared with his and my packs, the final few boys following. A sudden shower of sparks blew into the courtyard on the wind and an involuntary gasp of fear leapt from many mouths. The letter of the law loomed large: we had Duty of Care for a hundred teenagers as a bushfire advanced.

"Have we got a roll?" Tony bellowed at me above the fearful chatter.

"I don't know," I replied. "My roll got shredded along with most of the paperwork on Day One. What did you do with the orienteering rolls?"

"Maddy," Tony enjoined, as he ripped open the side of his pack. "Call the roll. Then you and Victoria start moving the kids down the track towards the highway." He pulled out papers and brandished three of them. "Bingo."

Maddy took the list, pulled a pen from her sleeveless pink vest pocket and began shouting names. The students answered. In a moment she had established the presence of all but Travis, Blake and Damien. The group needed no urging to leave.

"Stick together and stick to the track," Tony stipulated. "No running. It will take a while to get to the highway and even there we won't be safe. We can't let anyone stray from the group. We can't chase after anyone who wants to take a shortcut through an area that might go up in flames."

"What are we doing about Travis and co?" Victoria shouted.

"I'll wait for them," I said. "Until the last moment."

Tony regarded me searchingly. "Are you sure?"

I nodded, looking him in the eye. "We have Duty of Care."

He hesitated. "Don't do anything stupid."

"I won't," I replied.

"I'll take your pack," Tony acquiesced. "Don't let the fire get too close."

"I won't."

"Keep your water bottle."

Tony emptied the last of his water bottle into mine, as the group moved away from the doomed campsite. The area cleared. Tony was last to go.

"If they don't show up in fifteen minutes," he insisted, "Run for it."

"Don't worry. I'll catch you by the time you get to the highway."

In a moment the camp was empty. The wildlife had gone quiet. Suddenly, a large flock of rosellas flew over, heading South. I hurried up the path in the general direction from which the birds had flown. Pausing, the only sound was my puffing and blowing. Sudden sweat from my eyes almost made me miss seeing Damien, perched on a narrow branch in a young gum tree, face bleeding and contorted by fear.

"The fire's comin'," he exclaimed.

"Get down from there!"

"I can't. I'm scared."

"Damien, the fire will cook you if you stay there."

"I can't climb down. I can't hold on."

He showed me his hands, which were cut and bleeding from climbing in his haste to escape from Travis and Blake.

"Slide down the trunk. I'll catch you."

Smoke and sparks blew past. I felt the sting as a couple of them brushed my arm. My burns and cuts throbbed as the heat rose noticeably.

"Mr Moon … I'm scared –"

"Do it!" I yelled. "Now! I'll catch you."

The branch he sat on began breaking. Emitting a cry of terror, Damien slid from his perch and grabbed for the tree-trunk. He plummeted into my arms and we hit the hard ground together.

"Are you OK?" I shouted. More smoke and sparks showered us.

"I… think so…"

I swung his arm around my neck and helped him up.

"Come on. We need to catch up to the others," I urged. "Where are Travis and Blake?"

"I dunno," he grunted, face contorted. "Mr Moon...Trav, he's psycho. He stabbed me."

I could identify with that. Blood was already on my one remaining T-shirt. Damien's face wore a deep cut and his arm was bleeding as well. He began whimpering as we staggered in the direction of camp.

"What happened?"

"He took my tablets, drank the booze that he kept for him and Blake and smoked a lot of weed. I tried to stop him, but he went whacko and slashed at me with the knife. Blake held me and Trav cut my arms and chest. I kicked him in the balls and ran. I've been hiding in the bush. They came hunting me, but I hid in a little cave and they gave up."

The heat had intensified from the north and the heat haze became visible above the tree-line. Two of our charges were still out there.

"Come on, Damo," I said. "We have to hurry."

"Mr Moon," he said in a small voice. "I'm sorry."

"That's OK, Damo –"

"No, Mr Moon. I was a dick. I'm ... really sorry."

"OK," I said. "No worries, Damo. Now, come on."

I half-dragged him at the run after the group, shouting at the top of my lungs. As the path straightened, I could see Tony ahead, at the rear of the orderly retreat. Maddy turned and, still limping, rushed back up to the path.

"I found Damo," I shouted. I turned to him. "Go with the others."

"You're OK, Mr Moon," he said and hurried off.

"Where are the others?" Maddy demanded, as she reached me.

"I don't know."

"They can't be far. Let's give ourselves five minutes to find them."

I looked into her eyes. I could deny her nothing.

"OK."

We hurried together back to the campsite and the path that led in the direction of the ranger hut. The path forked. We looked at each other.

"I'll check this way," she gasped, pointing to the left. "You –"

My eyes indicated the other. "Five minutes," I panted. "Then –"

"Five minutes," she agreed.

The bush was tinder dry after a summer with no rain. Blast furnace heat struck me I ran hard up the slope, shouting the boys' names. Sheets of rampant fire leapt to the sky on the opposite ridge, the wind fanning it in my direction. Suddenly Blake appeared at the run. He saw me and stopped.

"That way!" I shouted, pointing him towards the path to the highway.

Blake hesitated, his face a study in conflicted emotions.

"Hurry!" I shouted. "Have you seen Travis?"

"I lost him," he yelled, looking back at the encroaching flames.

"Go! I'll see if I can find him!"

Blake started forward, paused, regarded me with wild-eyed astonishment, then a shower of sparks jump-started him down the path towards safety.

Friday, 9.10 a.m.

There was no sign of Maddy and the agreed five minutes had elapsed some time before. If Travis was ahead of me, he was already barbecued. Flames were already eating up bush to my right. The roar of the furnace filled my ears and a flash of pink caught my eye. I stopped and gaped in horror at Maddy's pink sleeveless vest, snagged on a low-lying branch.

I ran about the dormitories in a frenzy, shouting Maddy's name.

A wombat emerged from the enveloping smoke, waddling from behind the male dorm. Travis followed.

"Travis," I implored. "This has to stop."

"No way," he raged, waving his knife. He disappeared into the smoke.

"Travis!" I shouted, running after him. "Where are you?"

Leaping orange tongues of flame were on us. Surely Travis would turn around. The wind was fanning the fire towards the campsite. Smoke billowed more thickly around me. The wall of heat advanced.

Through the smoke haze there was a flash of colour.

"Maddy?" I bellowed. "Maddy?"

About fifty metres back, some stringybarks caught alight and the heat gained in intensity. There was Travis, surrounded by flames on three sides. I ran in. He slashed at me and I kicked his leg. He dropped the knife and clutched at his thigh.

"Owww...fucking arsehole! I'm tellin' Ferrier. You kicked me."

No prizes for guessing who would be in trouble with Ferrier.

Bad teaching, kicking a kid in the thigh after he threatened you with a knife without witnesses.

I grabbed him. He struggled madly in my grasp.

"Travis!" I shouted. "We've got to go."

"Fuck off!" he screamed. "I'm not goin' back. They'll put me in Juvie."

He turned and ran towards the fire.

Where was Maddy?

The heat intensified. I couldn't see Maddy and had no way of knowing whether she was alive. Travis was within reach and I had agonised over my repeat failures to bring him back to the fold. I rushed into the thick smoke, my T-shirt over my mouth. In a heartbeat I knew I was in mortal danger. I was about to turn and run for my life when I saw Travis, hemmed in by flames, collapsing to the ground. I ran through a blast of heat and dragged him to his feet. Again he struggled.

I sighed and hit him hard in the face. The fight left him long enough for me to pull his T-shirt over his nose and mouth to prevent him breathing too much smoke. Clear of the immediate flames, eyes smarting with heat and smoke, burns to my body silently screaming, I hauled Travis over my right shoulder. He thrashed about and screamed his extensive vocabulary of curses as I laboured back towards the camp courtyard. I dropped him into the dirt by the central campfire area, as a Country Fire Service truck roared into camp.

There was no sign of Maddy. In a nightmare of pain, mental and physical, I tore about the camp, in and out of the dorms, crying out her name. The fire was on top of us when the CFS men dragged me to the truck.

Friday, 12.30 p.m.

Fire had razed the bushland all around the campsite. The logistics of moving the kids to the town where I was made so unwelcome proved challenging, but one of the CFS men told me that two superannuated school buses had been mobilised. Travis and I arrived on the truck at the highway moments ahead of the bushfire.

We missed the second bus by several minutes and had to wait by the road while the uncontrolled furnace approached. Without his knife, bong and marijuana stash, smarting from the punch to the face, the kick to the thigh and having come down from his drug-induced mania, Travis curled up into an unresponsive ball and sulked. The promised lift to the town pulled up in a cloud of dust, the same ancient truck and weathered rustic who had helped me three days before.

"Don't suppose we'll be seein' our money too soon," he hazarded, before the booming forest fire precluded further pleasantries.

It occurred to me then that Doc's diary would have been lost to the fire. Victoria's car would be incinerated, likewise the earthly remains of Doc himself. In my private universe of horror, Maddy had roasted in the hellish flames. However, when I stepped down from the truck by the service station on the highway, there she was on the grass, minus her pink sleeveless vest, conducting the choir *a capella*. She smiled at me. Angels sang.

"Maddy! You're alive."

The song concluded and the kids relaxed in the grass, those whose batteries were not dead happily reunited with phone and internet connectivity.

"I got it," she said. The music in my soul missed a beat and faltered.

"Got what?"

"The job at Channel Nine. I'm off to Sydney."

"Huh?"

"Surely you knew," she added brightly. "I had been sweating on the news all week. You should see all my messages. I'm flying up tonight."

A black Mercedes appeared from the heat haze and pulled up. Maddy grabbed her bag, donned her sunglasses and waved to Victoria and Tony. I blinked ash and dust from my eyes with sudden tears.

"Maddy," Victoria cried, running to her and embracing her tearfully. "I can't believe you're going."

"It was on the cards," said Maddy, kindly.

"I'll miss you," Victoria sobbed. "I love you."

"Don't worry, Vicky," Maddy cooed and kissed her on the lips. "You'll find someone. I know you will."

"No-one like you," she wailed.

"Good luck, Maddy," said Tony. Cat-like, his pale green eyes slid in my direction and he nodded ever so slightly.

"I'll never see you again," I whispered. Maddy didn't hear me.

Her phone was ringing. The car door slammed and she swept from our lives, already engaged in the next step of hers. The Mercedes vanished from view. Victoria was weeping openly. Until that moment she had not entertained the possibility that Maddy would be snapped up by the Nine network as a musical mentor to up-and-coming network reality TV stars. But she was. It had happened.

"Suck shit," said Travis, suddenly next to me, left eye swollen closed.

Later, the buses from school nearly passed us by. The first driver, startled to see us waving from the roadside, confessed that he had only just learnt about the fire. Seeing the smoke, he had tuned into the radio news.

By the time we swung through the staff car park gates, the media was in position, clamouring for clarification. The hall was empty, delegates gone, just cleaners folding tables and mopping floors remained. The light was on in Ferrier's office, but the door was closed.

I checked my phone and noticed that Gaz had not called as promised.

Friday, 5.00 p.m.

We paid Naomi a visit in her office that afternoon. The conference's final crowning glory had been ruined by breaking media revelations of the Year Nine Camp disaster. Ron's terror of parental scrutiny into the facts of the fire had already snapped the Happy Vale lid down tight.

"Controlling that many kids on your own is impossible at the best of times," Victoria raged, having refashioned the shards of her broken heart into jagged blades of accusation.

"That's right," Naomi cut in spitefully. "Blame the kids, as always –"

"It was an emergency," Victoria seethed, pounding Naomi's desk.

"Managed badly," Naomi huffed.

"What were we supposed to do?" Victoria demanded.

"Supervise the students in a professional manner –"

"You accuse *us* of unprofessional conduct?" Victoria ranted. "If you had behaved professionally as Deputy Principal, you would have checked off every kid personally before letting them on the bus. You would have supported Peter, marking the roll and doing a head-count, especially since the other supervising teacher was absent. Travis and Damien should never have been able to sneak on that bus."

"That was not my responsibility," Naomi sniffed.

"Rubbish!" Victoria fumed.

"Five staff, one hundred kids," Tony accused. "Well outside the agreed teacher-student Outdoor Ed supervision ratio. You knew that."

"I don't have time for this." Naomi half-rose, attempting dismissal.

"You need to make time," Victoria fumed. Naomi sank back into her chair. "This is your fault. Your negligence led to Travis Armour and Damien Zammit, habitual troublemakers under current suspension, joining this camp to cause mayhem. Without them, there wouldn't have been a bushfire, caused by suspended stowaways smoking drugs."

"That's not the point," Naomi grated. "You failed in your duty of care!"

"How dare you?" Victoria snarled. "You failed in *your* duty of care. As our line manager, you failed *us*!"

"Where was our sixth teacher?" I demanded.

"We couldn't spare anyone," Naomi protested with injured innocence. She fixed me with a malicious stare. "Oh, and there's a charge against you for theft.

Apparently you stole a bicycle from a police officer. It was lost in the fire. Don't think the department or the law will excuse your larceny. And Travis tells me you assaulted him. You're in a lot of trouble."

My mouth opened, but no sound could make its way past the sudden roadblock in my throat.

"You must have known about Graham not paying the bills for his investment," Tony added coldly. "You must have known the place was unstaffed and locals out of pocket."

"I knew nothing of the sort," Naomi denied, furtive eyes averted.

"Why did no one confirm camp staff presence?" Tony demanded. "Parents had paid for activities that we couldn't deliver. What were we supposed to do?"

"That was your responsibility," Naomi accused.

"That was the responsibility of the designated Outdoor Ed teacher we didn't have," Victoria fumed. "We were just the seconded staff. Which part of our job description said we had to attend to booking details?"

"You had no part in the conference," Naomi scowled. "You wanted no part. Therefore, it was your responsibility –"

"That is bullshit and you know it, Naomi," Tony erupted, his customary calmness cracking. "As our line manager, it was your responsibility."

"I'm reporting you to the Regional Office for incompetence," Victoria hissed. "I say it to your face, Naomi Meredith. You are incompetent and unfit to administer a school. And I see Ferrier's not here. The irresponsibility is mind-boggling –"

"How dare you? You've done nothing but complain since your appointment –"

"You make me sick," Victoria hissed. "Doc is dead because of you."

"I refuse to listen to this –"

"Doc's death is directly related to your bloody-minded insistence that he do this camp against his doctor's orders," Tony concurred icily.

"He volunteered –"

"Hardly," Victoria interrupted. "You and Ferrier badgered him."

"He was a malcontent –"

"How anyone with a shred of conscience could be anything else in this establishment is beyond me," Victoria snapped.

"Your negligence led to Doc's death," Tony charged.

Naomi flushed scarlet, her breath coming in short gasps.

"Let it be on your conscience," Victoria breathed.

"How dare you?" Naomi exploded. "Get out of my office. I have nothing further to say to you."

"Oh," said Victoria. "You'll have to deal with us when we finally get an inquiry into this. You'd better have your facts straight. No one knows about Travis and Damien stowing away. We are going to redress that as soon as we leave you here. You've fucked up big time."

"Get out!" Naomi screamed, bursting into tears. "Get out!"

Four years later…

The phone call never came from Gaz. He was not at the pub that Friday. The beer went down pretty well and before long I was feeling no pain. When asked about the cut on my arm, not wanting to dwell on my ordeal I dismissed it as nothing in particular. The guys noted an absence of complaints about the northerlies and associated bullshit from school. Tony had advised me to keep the story quiet for the time being, which suited me very well.

When Gaz did not phone nor appear at the pub the following Friday, he became the conversational focus. Later, I heard of his unfortunate business decision to entrust a large sum of money to one Graham Fleming, whose eventual surfacing on a Mediterranean island with no extradition arrangement with Australia precluded any chance of financial recompense.

My classes were going quite well. When Annika Jones approached me in the yard - apropos of nothing in particular - and apologised for being a bitch, I had no words for her but a sudden lump in the throat. When Blake Sims asked me to help him through some information involving a career as a professional fisherman, I fought down my astonishment and helped him.

Then I remembered Doc's words:

I teach for that moment, for it is in that moment I am that young man with the divine spark and I can move mountains.

I'm not saying all my charges turned out well. That would be the province of fairy tales. Some kids take longer than others to learn. Some repent only on their deathbeds.

The next school newsletter waxed hyperbolic over the conference. EXTRA-licious northerlies prevailed. Maddy was restored to her former Princess Royal status in an effusive farewell, but the silence over the camp, the fire and Doc's demise might have done the *Politburo* proud in Stalin's heyday.

We hadn't reckoned with the small army of lawyers assigned to make the camp story go away, though. Tony, Victoria and I found ourselves in Ferrier's office soon enough, facing men in suits whose message was unequivocal: nothing happened, not even me hitting Travis. To dwell on such unpleasantness would be unhelpful to Affirmative Education.

Victoria's tireless agitation for blood had brought her to the attention of the authorities and also the union. She was seconded and rose rapidly to an executive position, a tireless advocate for the rights and well-being of the classroom teacher. Tony's incisive recount of the camp to his local Member of Parliament led to a meeting with the Education Minister and Tony receiving a very healthy early retirement payout that enabled him to set up his small business consultancy.

It also led to the prompt retirement of Ron Ferrier. Naomi Meredith disappeared from the radar altogether, until accounts emerged of her return to the classroom in the western suburbs and subsequent extended stress leave. Happy Vale High School found itself with a brand-new Admin team by July of that year. Hot northerlies still blew, but the new team also saw the need for an effective Behaviour Management system to back up Affirmative Education.

Year Nine remained without a coordinator until one of the new Assistant Principals noticed that Year Nines were responding well to my directions. She revealed later that Damien Zammit had been an advocate for me. He was backed by Blake Sims, with the rest of the class she was visiting at the time.

Travis Armour did his time in Juvenile detention. When he appeared out of the blue on my list for Year Twelve Drama three years later, it became clear he had always been interested in theatre lighting. His work in Drama led to an apprenticeship as a theatre technician. Something he said at the Year Twelve farewell dinner that year led to the legend of the teacher who cared enough to run through fire for his students. Then he apologised for being a dick in Years Eight and Nine.

And I forgave him.

THE END